Stolen

Memories

By:

J. A. Anderson

Published by Little House Publishing

ISBN-13: 978-0-6151-5213-4

This one is for Kimberly,

my daughter and best friend.

Many years of working in Geriatrics has afforded me an inside view of the devastation Alzheimer's Disease wreaks on its victims and their family members. This is one family's story. It is important to note that symptoms vary greatly from individual to individual.

Stolen Memories is a work of fiction. It is not meant to promote any method of care. And it goes without saying; any mistakes made are the responsibility of the author

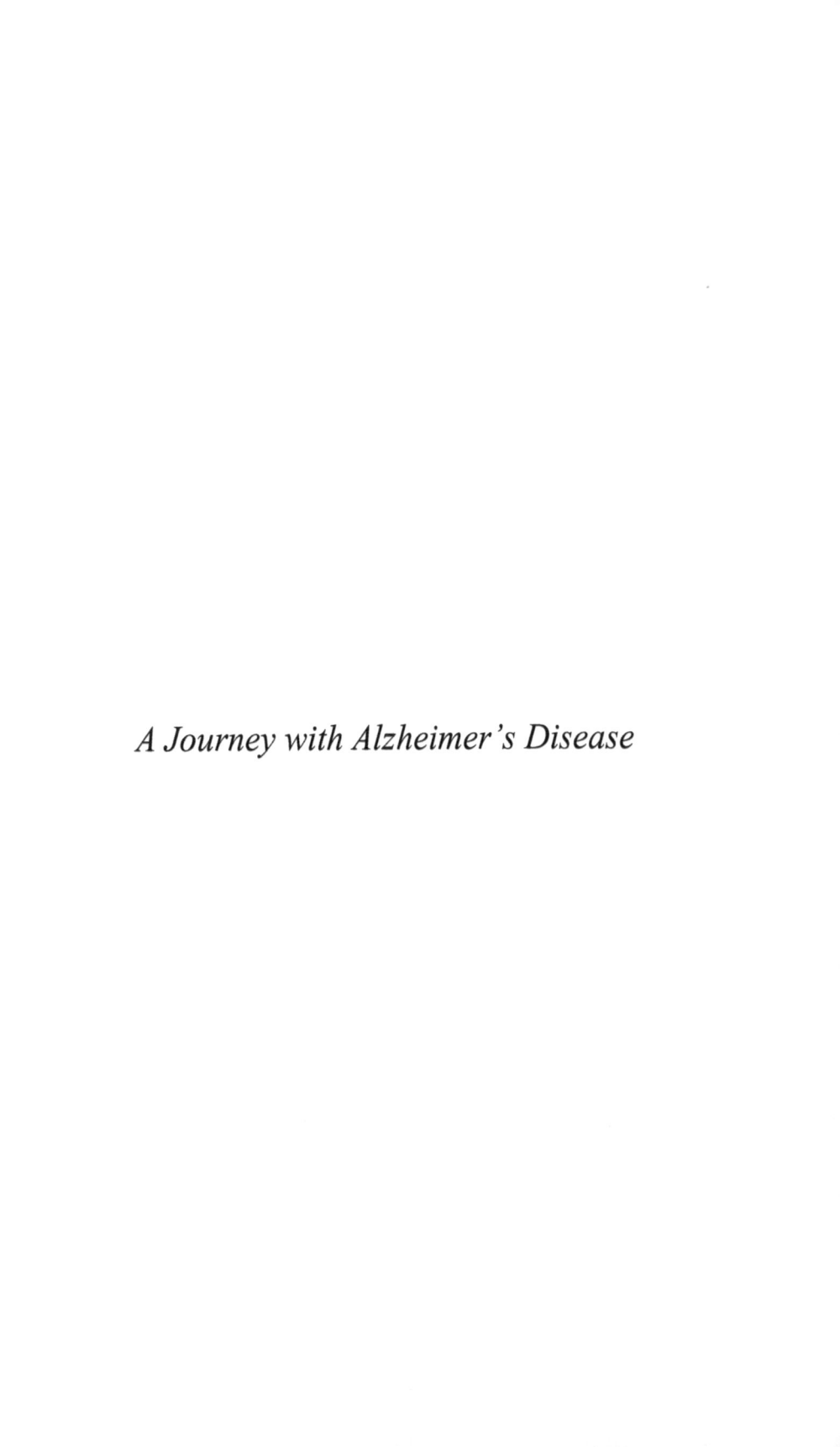

A Journey with Alzheimer's Disease

Part One

1

Maggie rubbed her eyes, hoping to erase the fuzziness of fatigue, and prayed that her mascara didn't smear. It was nearly five o'clock and John would soon be pulling into the driveway at home, while once again, she was stuck at the office. Where did the time go? There was still so much to do. The Jonsgaard account was hanging around her neck like a noose. She had been thrilled when Sheila had put her in charge of their ad campaign proposal, but now it was nothing but a migraine waiting to happen.

She glanced at her watch. John should be home by now. Her hand lingered on the telephone receiver. God, she didn't want to make the call. Thank goodness she had the foresight to throw a pot roast into the crock pot before she left home this morning. At least she wouldn't have to listen to John's lame complaints about eating frozen entrees again.

Maggie took a deep breath for courage and started to dial. Okay, now she knew she was tired. What the heck was her home phone number? She laughed at her own stupidity. Apparently, she didn't call herself often enough. Finally, after the third try, she was successfully connected with John.

"Hey Honey, it's me. I'm going to be a little late again. Go ahead and eat without me. I have a pot roast with potatoes and carrots cooking in the crock pot, just the way you like it."

"Really, well it might have helped if you had plugged it in. I'm not a huge fan of raw meat. Seriously Maggie, what is wrong with you lately?"

"You're kidding?" She paused, as a shiver snaked down her spine. "I'm sorry. It's this damn Jonsgaard account. I thought it would be a piece of cake, but I just can't seem to wrap my brain around it. Everything I've done so far is nonsense. I can't leave until I finish this proposal. We meet with the clients on Monday."

"You've been working late for the past two weeks. Don't get me wrong, I'm not complaining. Well, not much. But seriously, I'm starting to worry about you. I've never seen you so consumed by a project. Maybe you should talk to Sheila."

"Talk to Sheila? And say what? I'm sorry, I know this is a huge contract for the firm, but I'm an idiot and can't get the job done. Come on John, you know I can't do that. I promise, I'll finish up as soon as possible. I'm sorry about your dinner though. I'll make it up to you this weekend. Okay?"

John sighed. "Okay. I'm sorry too. I know your job is important, but I miss you. By the way, what am I supposed to eat for supper?"

Maggie chuckled. "Sometimes you're worse than a kid. Grab yourself a beer and order a pizza. I'll be home as soon as I can. Love ya"

"Love you too. Bye."

Maggie hung up the phone and stared at the piles of worthless paper on her desk. She lit a cigarette, ignoring the rule against smoking in the office, and prayed for inspiration.

~

Journal Entry

I have the Sunday afternoon blues and it is only Saturday. I feel like a kid, sent away for summer camp. How can you feel homesick when you are already at home? I hate the feeling, but I can't seem to shake it.

I have been too obsessed by work lately. I'm certain John would agree. He thinks Sheila is pushing too much work on me. I wish that was true. At least then I could make her the villain in this scenario. Unfortunately, that isn't the case. The Jonsgaard proposal should have been a few hours work. Yes, it is a big account, but it is a pretty routine deal. I finally finished up a little after midnight, but truth be told, I'm still not satisfied with it. Well, I'm not going to worry about it. Monday will come soon enough.

I would love to crawl on the couch with a sappy novel and forget about the rest of the world for a while. But, I promised John we would spend some time together this weekend. Poor baby, he is feeling neglected. I suppose I shouldn't complain, at least he misses me. Truthfully, I miss him too.

Maggie

~

It was a magnificent day for a picnic. Maggie leaned back on her elbows and tilted her face to the sun. Its gentle rays embraced her, while a gentle breeze tickled her skin. She inhaled the pleasing aroma of freshly cut grass and sighed. There was nothing finer than a spring day in Minnesota. It was warm enough for shorts, but it was still too early for the mosquitoes that Minnesotan's jokingly called the State bird.

The park was only five blocks from their house, yet she felt that she was in another world. It was still a thrill to watch the boats sailing on the mighty Mississippi River. An eagle flew overhead and she was enraptured by its majesty. It was a glorious day to be alive.

This was her favorite section of the park. It wasn't crowded, yet you could still hear the heartwarming sounds of children playing on the playground. It was a perfect moment in a perfect day, and if she had the power, she would stop the passing of time and savor it forever.

It was good to be away from the office, and all the headaches waiting for her there. Oh, she loved her job, or at least she used to, but ... she forced the unwelcome thought from her mind. She refused to worry about work now. She couldn't recall the last time she and John had taken time out from their hectic schedules for an afternoon alone, and she intended to enjoy every second of it.

"A penny for your thoughts." John whispered softly in her ear as he inhaled the gentle fragrance of her perfume. In his eyes, she was still the same beautiful young woman that captured his heart over forty years ago. His goals in life were simple, to love and protect this woman he cherished, and to savor every moment he could share with her. He treasured the sparkle of her sapphire eyes and the warmth of her smile melted his heart. Her beauty was not untouched by time, rather it was enhanced by it. The passing years had mellowed her and made her softer and if possible, even more desirable. She was the love of his life and his reason for living.

Maggie's heart quickened at the sound of his voice and the soft caress of his breath on her skin. He still excited her after all of the years they had shared together. She smiled and slowly opened her eyes, eager to embrace the sight of him. She loved to run her fingers through the thick silver hair that complimented the handsome, slightly lined face it crowned. She stared into the steel blue eyes that seemed to peer into her soul. They belonged to each other in so many ways. They were best friends, confidantes, soul mates, parents to their two children, and perhaps most important of all, lovers. They were partners for life, and Maggie smiled as she pondered the thought.

"You'd be wasting your money." She finally answered. "I wasn't thinking about anything except how much I love you."

John frowned. "And that isn't worth even a penny of my hard earned money? Woman, I am insulted."

Maggie teasingly pushed away from him and giggled. Good Lord, he could still make her feel like a school girl, and more importantly, a woman. "Oh, you know what I mean. I was just enjoying this gorgeous day."

John scanned the sky. "It's a nice one, that's for sure, but the fresh air and sunshine aren't doing anything to fill my growling stomach."

"Just like a man, always thinking about food. Hand me the picnic basket and we can eat."

"Okay. I'll open the bottle of wine while you get lunch ready."

Maggie emptied the basket and arranged their lunch on the blanket. It was a feast fit for a King. There were cold cuts and cheese, her famous fried chicken, fresh fruit and fudge brownies for dessert.

John handed her a plastic glass filled with red wine and appraised the spread with hungry eyes. "What, no potato salad?" He asked. "You always make potato salad for our picnics. You know it's my favorite."

Maggie frowned. "Of course, there's potato salad. I made it last night." She reached for the basket, and was shocked to find it empty. "I don't understand it. I must have forgotten to pack it. I'm sorry."

John dropped his head in mock despair. "Over forty years of picnics and this is the first without potato salad. Is this a sign of things to come? Don't you love me anymore?" John teased.

Tears welled in Maggie's eyes. The magic spell was broken. Logically, she knew her feelings were totally out of proportion with the situation, but she couldn't seem to control herself. The day was ruined and it was her fault. She gulped back an unwelcome sob. "I'm sorry. I don't know what is wrong with me lately. I guess I'm getting old and worn out."

"Hey now, stop it." John said as he wiped away her spilt tears. "I was only kidding. It's not a big deal. I didn't mean to hurt your feelings. There's enough food here to feed an army. Besides, if you're getting old, what does that make me? I've got a couple of years on you, remember?"

Maggie smiled. Perhaps he was right. It was hardly the end of the world.

So, why did it seem so important?

2

"Maggie, where the hell are my socks?" John called from the bedroom.

Maggie sighed and slapped her mascara wand down on the bathroom counter top. "Men, could God have created a more helpless creature?" She mumbled to herself. She stepped into the bedroom and found John, standing in his underwear, staring into his dresser drawer. His hands were balled into fists and placed defiantly on his hips. All four drawers were open wide and clothes were scattered across the bed and the floor.

Maggie viewed the mess and swore under her breath. "John, what the hell are you doing? I'm running late myself. I don't have time to dress you too."

"Damn it Maggie, I don't need you to dress me. I just want my freaking socks. I have a staff meeting at nine, I don't have time to play hide and seek."

"Well, I imagine they are in the same place they've been for the past forty years." She peered into his sock drawer and found it empty. They weren't anywhere in the mess of clothes scattered around the room. What the hell? Where could they be?

"John, if this is some kind of a joke, it isn't funny."

"Do I look like I'm laughing? Now, what did you do with my socks?"

"They have to be here. I just did laundry yesterday." She struggled to remember. "Maybe I left them in the dryer. I'll go check."

Maggie returned to the bedroom empty handed and more confused than ever. Frustrated, she turned to her dresser and tugged on the top drawer. It wouldn't budge. "What the heck...?" She grumbled. She forced the drawer open a crack and slipped her fingers into the tight opening. Holding down the overflow that was preventing the drawer from opening, she was finally able to pry it open. Balls of socks popped out of the drawer like a bunch of furry jack in the boxes.

John laughed in spite of himself. The look on Maggie's face was priceless. "Now, why didn't I think to look there?" He grabbed a pair of socks and left the room still chuckling to himself.

Maggie picked up a pair of socks and stared into the drawer. It didn't make any sense. Why would she cram John's socks into her underwear drawer? If she didn't know any better, she would suspect someone was playing a cruel joke on her. But, she couldn't cast the blame onto anyone else. There was no denying she had been a little distracted lately. Well, she didn't have time to worry about that now. She gathered John's socks and carefully placed them in their appropriate drawer, double-checking just to make sure they were really there. Glaring at the scattered clothes with disgust, she decided they would have to wait. There was no time to put them away now.

John found her and pecked her cheek good bye. "Perhaps you should think about dyeing your hair blonde." He teasingly suggested.

Maggie forced herself to share his joke. She laughed, though tears were threatening to fall. The humor in the situation escaped her.

She returned to the bathroom and hastily completed applying her make-up. Thank God, she remembered to do that. She would have looked real fine, going to work with one eye done. She did a quick double check in the mirror, just to make sure she was completely dressed. Nothing would surprise her anymore.

Feeling a little paranoid and unsure of herself, she walked through the house to make sure everything was turned off. Finally, satisfied that the house wouldn't burn down in her absence, she grabbed her purse and headed for the door.

She reached into her purse and couldn't find her keys. "Damn, I don't need this today." She grumbled to herself and began a frenzied search of the house, becoming more desperate with each passing moment. Maggie glanced at her watch and gasped. She was late. It was the first time in over twenty years. Damn John and his stupid socks. She sighed in frustration, and caught her reflection in the mirror on the wall. Her keys were dangling from her mouth. Tears of relief and embarrassment filled her eyes. Thank goodness John wasn't there to witness her latest feeble-minded performance. He would never let her live it down and frankly, his jokes were beginning to wear on her already frazzled nerves. But, she had to admit; she was certainly turning into a scatterbrain.

An hour later, Maggie was finally seated, safely behind her desk. She was still shaken by her hectic morning, but she was determined to put it behind her. Everyone has a bad day every now and then, she assured herself, and she was making way too much of some misplaced socks and keys. The day was bound to get better. She busied herself with some overdue files and the rest of the morning seemed to fly by. Satisfied, that she managed to accomplish something constructive, she was ready for lunch.

A sharp rap on the door interrupted her plans. "Come in." Maggie called. Sheila, her immediate supervisor and long time friend, poked her head inside the door. "Maggie, can I see you in my office for a moment please?"

"Sure, I was just going to lunch. I'll stop in when I get back." Maggie answered.

"No. Now." Sheila demanded and closed the door.

Maggie's heart began to pound, rushing blood echoed in her ears. Calm down, she told herself. I'm overreacting again. Sheila seems upset, but I've never had a problem with her before, and I can't imagine what might be wrong. There was no need to panic, at least until she found out what this was all about.

Maggie forced herself to stand on trembling legs and walked the long hallway to Sheila's office. Her heels sunk in the plush carpet, making her feel as though she were walking in quick sand. The secretary wasn't at her desk and Sheila's door stood ajar. Maggie gathered her courage, knocked softly and entered.

She forced herself to meet Sheila's gaze. "You wanted to see me?"

"Close the door and sit down Maggie."

Maggie cleared her throat, yet her squeaking voice surprised her. "Is something wrong Sheila? I'm, terribly sorry I was late this morning, but it has never happened before and I didn't think it would be that big of a deal. After all, it was the first time in over twenty years."

Sheila's left eyebrow lifted just a fraction of an inch. "This has nothing to do with being late, and to be honest, I didn't even realize you were, although that might explain a few things." She paused for just a second. "Maggie, where were you at ten thirty this morning?"

"I was at my desk, finishing some reports. Why?"

"Does the Jonsgaard contract mean anything to you?"

"Of course it does. We've worked months to set up that meeting." Maggie stopped short. Dear God, what day was it. She struggled to think. It wasn't possible. She couldn't have forgotten the meeting. It was too ridiculous to consider. She'd worked endless hours on that project, she wouldn't, couldn't, forget it. Yet, she must have.

"I missed the meeting, didn't I? Oh God. I am so sorry." She dropped her head in shame. She couldn't bear to face Sheila's disappointed stare. "I have no excuse. I don't know what to say."

The ominous sound of Sheila's pencil tapping the desk was the only sound in the room. It was hard to believe that a Ticonderoga pencil could evoke such a nerve-shattering clamor. Maggie fidgeted in her chair, feeling every bit as intimidated as a naughty child dispatched to the principal's office.

Maggie watched as Sheila's private storm brewed and was surprised to realize how much her perfectly arched eyebrows and meticulously applied make-up disturbed her. It was if she were staring at a Barbie doll in need of a face-lift. Sheila didn't seem real, but then again, this entire situation was surreal. Perhaps it was all a dream and she would wake up, safe and sound in her own bed. Unfortunately, Sheila's harsh voice startled her back to reality.

"Maggie, you and I have worked together for a long time. Perhaps I could understand this if you were new to the firm, but that isn't the case. You of all people know how important this contract is to this company. I suppose I could have reminded you about the meeting, but we just discussed it on Friday and I've always been able to count on you before."

All too familiar tears spilled down Maggie's cheeks. Crying had become a bad habit lately. "I know it doesn't solve anything, but I am so sorry. What can I do to make it up to you and the company? Sheila, I don't want to beg, but I will if I have to. You know how much I love my job. I hope this doesn't mean I have to leave."

Sheila shook her head. "Maggie, I'll be honest with you. If this happened to anyone else, I wouldn't hesitate to show them the door. However, you have been a valuable employee for too many years and I'm not prepared to lose you. But," she paused for effect, "this won't be without repercussions. I want you to hand over the Jonsgaard file. You are off that project permanently."

Maggie nodded. She wasn't surprised. "I understand. I'll give it to your secretary right away."

"Very good. And Maggie, let's try to put this behind us. You made a mistake. Granted, it was a whopper, but we're all human and life goes on. Why don't you take the rest of the day off. You can start fresh tomorrow."

Maggie somehow managed a feeble smile. "Thank you. I think I'll take you up on that."

Sheila stood. It was a sure signal that the meeting was over. "Okay, I'll see you tomorrow ... On time."

Maggie winced at the reminder of her tardiness, and stood to leave. She wanted to crawl back to her office. Was it her imagination, or was everyone staring at her? She was dripping in sweat and humiliation by the time she reached her desk.

So far, it had been a hell of a day

3

Dear God, please ease this tightening in my chest. I can barely catch my breath. What is happening to me? My life is good. I have a loving husband, two wonderful children, three beautiful grandchildren and a home that I love. These are supposed to be the "Golden" years, aren't they? If that's so, why do I seem to have this black cloud hovering over me?

Am I being punished for something? If I were superstitious, I'd wonder if perhaps a black cat crossed my path, or maybe I carelessly strolled beneath a ladder, but I've never believed in any of that hocus-pocus. Whatever the reason, or the cause, I pray this curse of bad luck has ended. I don't know how much more I can endure.

It's possible I'm making a mountain out of a series of molehills. If I look at each incident separately, they don't seem that significant. Forgotten salad, misplaced socks and a really bad day at the office aren't major tragedies by any stretch of the imagination. Yet, they've left me with a crushing weight on my chest and I feel as though I am drowning.

How can I possibly show my face in the office tomorrow? I've never felt so humiliated. I can still feel the accusing stares of my coworkers burning a hole in my back. I'm sure I was the topic of discussion all afternoon. I know it will fade in time, but how long will I have to suffer until another juicy tidbit of office gossip replaces my shame?

I don't want to tell John, but I've never hidden anything from him before. I wonder how he will react? Will he be mad? Will he think I'm becoming senile? I'm beginning to wonder myself. But, I really need his strong shoulder. I crave the comfort of his arms.

Perhaps I'm simply growing old, but I don't feel old. I've never thought of sixty-two as being old in the grand scheme of things. I try to take good care of myself. Well, besides an occasional cigarette and drink, but I read somewhere that wine can be good for your heart. I exercise, probably not as much as I should, but I'm not planning on running a marathon any time soon. I try to eat right, well outside of desserts, but everyone knows that chocolate is a major food group. Okay, admit it Maggie, you're hardly a health guru. Maybe I should start taking some of that ginseng stuff they advertise on television to improve my memory.

Sheila is right. I need to put this behind me. I made a mistake. I've finally proven that I'm human. Ha! Tomorrow can be a new beginning if I allow it to be. I'll be good as new after a good night sleep.

Thank you dear friend for listening. I would be lost without the comfort of your pages.

Until next time,

Maggie

~

Journal Entry

     I finally gathered up the courage to tell John about the fiasco at work. I'm not sure why I was so frightened to tell him. He isn't my boss and it isn't any skin off his nose if I make a mistake at work. To be honest, I guess his blonde jokes are beginning to wear on my nerves and I just didn't want to give him any more ammunition.

     To his credit he didn't make any sarcastic remarks. He did his best to comfort me. He said the right words to calm my fears and doubts, but I didn't buy it. His voice seemed to lack conviction and he seemed almost hesitant to offer his support.

     Dear God, now I'm not only absentminded, I'm paranoid too.
Maggie

~

Journal Entry

     Katie called me this morning. I realize that is hardly a newsworthy event. We talk on the phone nearly every day, but this was a very troubling conversation. And to be honest, I'm not sure who I'm more upset with, her or John.

     I can't believe John actually told her about the problem I had at work, last week. I suppose he has told Michael too. He might as well take out a front page ad in the paper, MY WIFE IS AN IDIOT! Believe me, he is going to hear about this. The kids don't have to know the details of our private lives. It is none of their business. Besides, I don't appreciate John talking about me behind my back.

Katie carried on as if forgetting an appointment was the end of life as we know it. She all but accused me of becoming senile. God bless her. She has a good heart, and I realize she is just concerned, but it makes me wonder what John told her.

I made it a point to remind her that I was the parent and she was the child in our relationship. I was pretty stern, and I'm sure I made her angry, but it had to be said. I refuse to be treated like a child or a senile old woman. At any rate, she'll get over it. She always does.

For the life of me, I can't imagine why everyone is making such a big deal out of this? I made a mistake, and there's no denying it was a whopper, but it is over now. I've worked at the same company for over twenty years and I have a darn good record with them. No one seems to remember that though. Besides, everything worked out in the end. My company still got the contract.

I just want to forget the entire ugly incident. And I certainly wish everyone else would too.

Maggie

4

"John, would you please hurry up and get dressed. They'll be here any minute and they don't need to see you running around in your underwear."

John laughed. "Maggie, would you settle down. It's just the kids. They've seen me in my boxers a thousand times."

"I know, and I've worked too hard on this meal to have their appetites ruined by the sight of your spindly legs. Now, go put some pants on." She playfully swatted his bottom with a dish towel and watched him walk into the bedroom. His legs were far from spindly. At sixty-five, John was still in great shape.

After a few minutes he returned to the kitchen, fully dressed and smiling. He casually massaged Maggie's shoulders and tenderly kissed her neck. "It seems to me that you've gone to an awful lot of trouble for a kid's birthday party."

"I know, but you're only five once. I can hardly believe it. Jacob is growing up so fast. It seems like only yesterday that Katie called to tell us she was pregnant."

John chuckled heartily. "I'll never forget that phone call. She was a wreck. She scared the hell out of me. I was sure by the way she was crying that something terrible had happened."

Maggie laughed in agreement. "Well, in her mind it was terrible. Jacob wasn't exactly a planned bundle of joy. Marcia was already eight and Lonnie was ten. They thought their family was complete."

"Remember, how worried she was about telling Craig? She was so sure he would be angry with her." John asked.

Maggie smiled at the memory. "I remember, but I knew better, and I was right. Craig was thrilled, and you know Katie wouldn't trade Jacob for anything on earth."

"I just wish there was a way to keep him this age. Lonnie and Marcia make me nervous. They seem too grown up for their own good. If you ask me, Marcia is far too young to be wearing that paint all over her face. And the thought of Lonnie behind the wheel of a car terrifies me."

Maggie sympathetically rubbed John's arm. "It's just growing pains Grandpa. Have you forgotten what Katie and Michael were like at that age? Let's just be grateful it's Katie and Craig's problem and not ours."

"Oh believe me, I am. Is there anything I can help you with?"

Maggie scanned the kitchen. "No, I think everything is under control. What time is Michael coming?"

John opened the refrigerator door and stared inside. He grabbed a beer and leaned against the counter. "He said he would be here in time for the game and that starts at one."

Maggie pointed to the beer can. "Just remember, this is Jacob's day."

"Yes dear." John meekly smiled, the picture of an innocent little boy.

It was heartwarming to have the entire family under one roof again. Michael's visits were few and far between. His long hours at the hospital saw to that. But it was a sacrifice he had to make and they were so proud of his accomplishments. It just made the time they had together sweeter. Besides, Maggie loved the sound of "my son the doctor", and she made it a point to introduce the phrase into conversation at every opportunity.

The grandchildren started to quarrel amongst themselves almost immediately, and John looked fairly frazzled within the first half hour, but Maggie was enjoying every chaotic minute of it. A house needs the sound of children to make it a home, and it was always better when it was someone else's children. At least they would leave eventually, Maggie thought to herself and smiled.

The meal was delicious and the conversation was lively. Michael had everyone in stitches with his wild anecdotes from the hospital. Of course, Jacob was chomping at the bit to open his presents, while Lonnie and Marcia argued about everything and nothing at all. Maggie watched it all, happy they were all together, yet remnants of anger still lingered. These were the same people that were talking behind her back just a couple of weeks ago and she still felt betrayed. But she wouldn't let it show. They would never know how much they hurt her.

Finally the dinner dishes were cleared, and it was time for dessert. Jacob voted against a traditional birthday cake in favor of an apple pie this year. He loved his Grandma Maggie's apple pie.

Maggie carefully placed five candles in the golden pie crust and set the pie in front of Jacob. The family joined voices and sang a slightly off key version of Happy Birthday in his honor. Jacob giggled, squeezed his eyes shut, made a secret wish and blew out the candles on his first try. Everyone clapped and cheered as if it was the greatest accomplishment of the century.

"John, would you get the ice cream while I serve the pie?" Maggie asked.

"Sure, but can I have cheese with mine?"

Maggie laughed. "Yes. Believe it or not I didn't forget. Your cheddar cheese is already sliced in the refrigerator."

"Cheese for me too Dad." Michael called out.

Maggie smiled at Katie. "Like father, like son."

Maggie scooped out generous portions of ice cream onto everyone else's plate. Of course, Jacob received the first serving. "The birthday boy gets his first." She announced.

Jacob licked his lips and dug into his pie with the gusto of a hungry five year old. He scooped a huge spoonful into his mouth and began to chew. His mouth puckered as his eyes popped open and he began to cough. He promptly spit the pie back out onto his plate.

Katie jumped out of her chair. As soon as she realized Jacob wasn't in any danger of choking, her concern turned to anger. "Jacob, what in the world is wrong with you? You know better than to take such a huge bite. That was very rude. Now, apologize to your grandma."

"I'm sorry Mom." Jacob whispered. "But the pie is yucky."

Katie blushed from embarrassment. "Don't be ridiculous." She scolded. "You were just making a pig out of yourself." She tasted a small forkful to prove her point. She winced slightly as her mouth puckered. She quickly spit the pie into her napkin.

Maggie watched with a growing sense of anxiety. Her pulse quickened and it was hard to catch her breath. Suddenly, all eyes were on her.

"Mom, what did you do to the pie? We can't possibly eat this." Katie asked.

Maggie caught the tone of accusation in her daughter's voice and panicked. "I don't know." Maggie stammered. "It's the same recipe I've used for years. I can't imagine..." She tasted a small sample herself. Bitterness assaulted her tongue and she knew immediately what must have happened. She raced into the kitchen and opened her sugar canister. She pinched a few granules between her fingers and tasted. It was just as she suspected. It was salt.

Tears filled her eyes and she succumbed to her out of control emotions. Her legs crumpled and she collapsed onto the floor, sobbing uncontrollably. What was happening to her? It seemed as though she couldn't do anything right anymore. Suddenly, everything seemed so difficult. She couldn't even bake a simple apple pie.

John followed Maggie into the kitchen and watched in horror as she crumbled to the floor. At that moment, a spoiled apple pie was the last of his worries. Something was terribly wrong.

He lowered himself to the floor and cradled Maggie in his arms. She seemed so small and defeated. It made his heart ache. This was the woman he loved more than life itself. Yet, she wasn't the same woman he thought he knew so well. His Maggie could work a full-time job, run a household and bake an apple pie with her eyes closed. And if by chance, a disaster like this occurred, and there had been a few through the years, she would be the first to laugh about it. Maggie wasn't afraid of poking fun at herself. But, she wasn't laughing now. And John realized, with a heavy heart, she hadn't been laughing for quite some time.

"Oh John," Maggie sobbed. "It was salt."

"What?" John asked, not quite understanding.

Maggie choked back a sob and struggled to find her voice. "I used salt instead of sugar in the pie. It's all my fault. I've ruined everything with my stupidity ... Again."

John brushed the hair from her forehead and gently wiped the tears from her cheeks. "Oh Honey." He soothed. "You haven't ruined anything. We had a fantastic dinner and Jacob can open his gifts. The important thing is that we're all together. Please, don't worry so much. It isn't worth your energy." Besides, he thought to himself, I'm worried enough for both of us.

Katie poked her head in the doorway, shocked to find both of her parents sitting on the floor. "Is everything okay in here?" She asked, even though it obviously wasn't. Her mother had streaks of mascara streaming down her face and her father looked downright scared. She suspected correctly that there was more going on in her parents lives than a spoiled apple pie.

Maggie buried her face in John's shoulder. God, she didn't want Katie to see her like this. "Everything is fine." John answered, perhaps just a little too quickly. "Your mother is just upset about the pie. Why don't one of you run to the store and pick up a cake or something for dessert. Let's get this party back on track." He said with an unconvincing smile.

Katie nodded and reluctantly left her parents alone. What was going on? She couldn't remember the last time she saw her mother cry and it was a disturbing sight. She was always so strong and capable. She joined the others and quietly explained the situation to Michael and Craig so the children wouldn't hear. Thank God she had Craig to lean on. He was a good and caring husband and an excellent father. It didn't surprise her when he volunteered to go to the store for dessert.

John and Maggie rejoined the party a few moments later. Katie noticed her mother's freshly scrubbed face and red rimmed eyes and her heart sank. Everyone smiled and put up a good front for the children's sake, but there was a tension in the air that was impossible to disguise.

Craig returned with a cake from the bakery and Katie took over the role as hostess without hesitation. Jacob opened his gifts and was thrilled with all of them. Of course, it was still fairly easy to please a five year old. The apple pie wasn't mentioned again. The festive atmosphere had disappeared as quickly as a popped balloon and everyone was anxious to escape. It was a relief to everyone when the party ended.

Maggie was exhausted and meekly excused herself to retire to the bedroom. The afternoon seemed to drag on forever and she was sure she wasn't imagining the strange looks from Katie and Michael. She just wanted to crawl into her warm bed and collapse. She didn't have the strength to even worry about it.

Meanwhile, John poured himself the first of a few strong drinks and sat alone in the solitude of his den. A thousand thoughts ran through his mind, and none of them were reassuring.

5

Another day, and another new beginning. I wonder how many I'm allowed. I've certainly managed to use up a fair share of them lately. My luck has to turn around pretty soon, doesn't it?

Poor Jacob. I'll never forget the look on his face when he bit into that pie. A few years ago I would have laughed it off, but now it is just one more shame I have to bear.

Sunday started out to be such a lovely day. It was so good to have everyone home again. I would have liked to spend more time with Michael, but I managed to ruin that opportunity too. Everyone was pretty anxious to hightail it out of here, and I guess I can't blame them. I made a pretty dramatic scene over the pie. I just can't seem to control myself. There seems to be a floodgate of tears, hiding behind my eyes, just waiting for the opportunity to spill.

I can tell John is starting to worry about me, and to be honest, I'm beginning to scare myself. I've thought about it a lot, and I'm convinced this is all related to the change of life. My hormone replacement medication probably needs to be adjusted. That makes sense, doesn't it? It would certainly explain the sudden mood swings and surplus of tears lately. I'll make an appointment to see my doctor, the first chance I get.

I feel better already.

Maggie

~

Several weeks passed without incident and Maggie was determined to put all the unpleasantness behind her. She was confident the black cloud that had been hovering above her had finally moved on. She glanced at her watch with pleasant anticipation. She had the afternoon off and was looking forward to a luncheon date with Katie. They planned on going shopping after lunch and Maggie was eager to spend some quality time with her daughter. She wouldn't admit it to Katie, but she was relieved the kids were all in school and wouldn't be joining them. Shopping with two teenagers and a five year old, just wasn't her idea of a good time.

Maggie walked into the restaurant and was shocked to see Katie already seated in a booth. Maggie grinned and waved. She made a point to check her watch before she sat down. "I can't believe you're already here. I've never known you to be on time for anything."

"I know. It's a terrible habit and it drives Craig crazy, so I promised him I would try harder. I'm turning over a new leaf. Just call me Prompt Patty."

Maggie laughed. "Well, I like it Patty. Keep up the good work. So, how have you been, and Craig and the kids?"

"We're all fine Mom." She leaned slightly forward. "How are you doing?"

Maggie straightened her back and sighed. Here we go, she thought to herself. She was hoping to have a pleasant day without any worries or hassles. She had no intention of defending herself to Katie, or anyone else for that matter. "I'm fine Katie." She answered in a firm voice that she hoped made it clear that the topic of apple pie or any other problems were off limits.

Katie threw up her hands in surrender. Message received. "Okay." She relented, willing to let the subject drop, at least for the time being.

The rest of the afternoon passed quickly. Katie did most of the talking and was eager to vent her lighthearted complaints about Craig's crazy work schedule and his sloppy habits, the trials and tribulations of trying to raise two teenagers and the energy it took to chase after a five year old. Maggie listened with interest and delight. Her daughter had grown into a remarkable woman and she was proud to be a part of her life.

Every store they entered seemed to have sales they couldn't possibly resist. They both spent more money than they intended to, but they laughed and convinced themselves they were saving money by taking advantage of all the bargains.

At the end of the day, they parted, feeling a little closer to each other, and grateful for the time they shared. They promised to get together more often. After all, life was too short.

6

Life was good. The sun was shining and the birds were singing an especially melodic song. The work week was over and Maggie had nothing planned for the next two days. She considered catching up with some housework, or maybe she would sit down and read the book she bought on her shopping trip with Katie. Perhaps she would be ambitious and do them both, or maybe she would be lazy and do neither. Either way, it sounded like the perfect weekend and she smiled in pleasant anticipation.

She made a small detour on her way home from work and picked up a bottle of wine. An intimate candle lit dinner might be nice Saturday evening, and who knew where that might lead. An unrecognizable sung hummed from her lips as she approached their front door. She was shocked to see John's car parked in the driveway so early on a Friday afternoon, but it was a pleasant surprise and it just added to her festive mood.

She juggled her packages and opened the front door, shocked to find John standing in front of her. Her gaiety quickly faded when she noticed the scowl on his face. His blue eyes were blazing. He stared at her with a look in his eyes that made the hair on Maggie's neck stand on end. A shiver ran down her spine. John seldom lost his temper and she couldn't recall a time when she had seen him so visibly angry. Even worse, his anger appeared to be directed towards her and she didn't have a clue as to why.

She struggled to remain calm. There must be a logical reason for this. "Hi Honey. What brings you home so early today?"

John didn't speak. Instead, he shoved a piece of paper in her face in response.

Maggie reached for the paper with a trembling hand. She read the letter and gasped. It was an overdraft notice from the bank. There had to be some kind of a mistake. They had never bounced a check in all the years they were married. Even when they were struggling newlyweds, John insisted the checking account was balanced to the penny. Watch your pennies and the dollars will take care of themselves, was his motto.

"Can you explain this to me Maggie?"

Maggie stared at the paper in disbelief. She didn't know what to say. "John, there has to be some kind of mistake." She reached into her purse and retrieved her checkbook. She examined the register and it clearly showed a balance of well over four hundred dollars. Feeling vindicated, she held out her checkbook as proof. "See, the bank must have made a mistake. This proves we're not overdrawn."

John snatched the checkbook from her trembling hand, glanced at it briefly, and tossed it to the floor. "I don't know what kind of mumbo-jumbo you have recorded in there, but it's bullshit. I thought there must have been a mistake too, so I ran a computer printout of our account and it shows there hasn't been a deposit made in over a month. Where are the deposits Maggie?"

They're in the bank. They have to be. You know I go to the bank every Friday morning to deposit the money into my household account." She hesitated for a moment. Today was Friday. She went to the bank this morning. Didn't she? She struggled to remember, but couldn't. Of course, she did. She must have. Panic gripped her. It was possible she forgot, maybe once, but certainly not for over a month.

"Okay Maggie, show me your deposit receipts then. If you have them, I can go back to the bank and get this mess straightened out." John challenged.

Maggie reached into her purse. "I know I have them here somewhere." She said, praying it was true. She pulled out fistfuls of gum wrappers and empty cigarette packs. She was shocked by the mess, and ashamed to display it in front of John. But, she continued to sift through the garbage, desperate to find the deposit slips that would prove her innocence. Finally, at the very bottom of the purse, she found several wrinkled and torn checks. Her heart caught in her throat. How could she possibly explain this? It was impossible. She forgot, and that was no excuse.

John snatched the checks from her hand and glared at her with an unsettling mixture of anger and confusion. "Maggie, can you imagine how embarrassing this was for me? I'm vice-president of the bank for Christ's sake. Of course, the bank covered our checks, so at least we're saved that embarrassment, but we'll still have to pay the service charges. They offered to waive them, but I won't accept any more favors from them. It wouldn't look right. Besides, we have to pay for our mistakes just like everyone else. I guess my biggest mistake was to think you could handle the household account. What the hell is happening to you?"

"I don't know ... I'm sorry." Maggie stammered. There was nothing to say. She was suddenly tired, weary to the bone. She didn't have the strength, or the ammunition to fight him. Tears slipped down her face as she hung her head in shame.

"Well, I know one thing for sure..." John said as bent to pick up the discarded checkbook off the floor. "This won't happen again." He shook the checkbook balefully in front of her face. "Because, you won't have this any more. I'll take care of all the banking from now on. I'll give you a cash allowance and you can do your shopping with that. Oh, and while we're at it, give me your credit cards. You won't be needing them any longer."

Maggie choked back a sob. This was without a doubt the most humiliating moment in her life. She could survive an argument with John, but this was different. She had lost his trust, and she was devastated. Yet, she couldn't blame him. She handed over her credit cards. They meant nothing to her. They were nothing but meaningless pieces of plastic. John's love and faith in her was all that mattered. Now, it seemed that was shattered, all because of her forgetfulness. She ran to the safety of her bedroom, unable to face his anger or disappointment a moment longer.

~

Journal Entry

I don't understand what is happening to me. I've never felt so lost and confused. Life used to be so simple. Now, it seems the world, my world at least, has turned topsy-turvy and I can't seem to get my bearings. I'm not sure which way is up, but sadly I understand downhill too well. Everything seems increasingly difficult, even the simplest task is complicated. My desk at work is plastered with sticky notes, written reminders for almost every move I have to make to get through the day. They would probably help if I remembered to read them.

I don't blame John for being angry with me. The bouncing checks must have been a mortifying experience for him, but I think he has blown this totally out of proportion. Granted, I made a mistake, another one, but he has to realize I have been under a lot of stress lately. Why can't he try to be more understanding? Screaming at me and taking the checkbook away doesn't solve the problem. I need his help, not his accusations.

I can't erase the image of John's angry face from my mind. I can picture it so clearly. His face was red from rage, the veins in his neck were so prominent, I could literally see his pulse. I pray I never have to be the target of that kind of ire again. Truly, I don't blame him. I'm angry with myself as well, but to be honest, I'm more sad and scared. This is terribly frightening. It's as if I'm fighting an invisible enemy and he is holding all the weapons, leaving me weak and vulnerable.

Sleep evades me. I lay in bed at night, exhausted, but unable to sleep. John seldom comes to bed with me. He stays up, well into the night. His footsteps echo in the silent house and I hear him sneak into the bedroom to check on me. I play possum and pretend to sleep. I can hear his muffled voice, more than likely talking to Katie and Michael on the phone. I am sure he is updating them on the latest escapades of their deranged mother. Why is he trying to turn my children against me?

Maggie

7

Maggie yawned deeply and reached for her cup of hot black coffee. The sleepless nights were starting to take their toll. At least things seemed a bit better with John, although she still felt as though she was walking on egg shells around him. But, she was doing her best to prove herself to him and assure him that she was still worthy of his trust and, most importantly, his love. It wasn't easy. She didn't even feel like herself any longer, and the pressure of her Oscar deserving performance was beating her down.

Maggie thumbed through the open file on her desk. She read the first paragraph for the third time and it still made no sense to her. The words may as well have been written in Latin. Frustrated, she removed her reading glasses and pinched the bridge of her nose. A dull headache was threatening to explode into a full blown migraine. Thankfully, her top drawer served as a personal pharmacy. She reached into the drawer and grabbed a bottle of Ibuprofen. Did she already take some? She shrugged her shoulders and popped three into her mouth and washed them down with her cooling coffee.

The telephone intercom buzzed. Maggie jumped at the sound. She stared at the machine. What in the world? What was that sound? Suddenly, a voice sounded through the speaker. "Maggie, are you there?"

It was Sheila's voice. Maggie's heart started. She leaned forward and talked into the machine, unsure if she would be heard. "Yes, I'm here."

"Good. I'm glad I caught you in your office. I'd like to talk to you. Come to my office in ten minutes."

Maggie's heart fluttered and her arm pits immediately dampened from perspiration. It wasn't a good day to forget the deodorant. What was wrong this time? She had been so careful to double and triple check everything she did. There couldn't be anything wrong, but she knew, without a doubt, something was.

The hands on the wall clock seemed to move faster than normal and the tick-tock echoed in her ears. The bewitching hour had arrived. She put on fresh lipstick as an afterthought and began the long walk down the carpeted corridor to Sheila's office once more. Dead man walking.

The secretary was at her desk. Maggie approached Doris and cleared her throat. "Hello Doris, Sheila wanted to see me. Is she ready?"

Doris became very busy with the stacks of paper on her desk. She simply nodded and kept her focus on the tasks in front of her. The lack of eye contact just confirmed Maggie's worst fears. Office gossip spread like wildfire, Maggie was probably the last to know about this supposed impromptu meeting. She knocked on Sheila's door and slowly entered.

A strange sense of déjà vu crept over her. She had played this scene before and she didn't like the plot. A lump formed in her throat, and for a moment, she feared she might choke. Her feet moved on their own volition. Perhaps this time would be different, but she was certain she wasn't there to accept the employee of the month award. The expression on Sheila's confirmed this wasn't a friendly visit.

Sheila motioned to the guest chair strategically placed in front of her desk. The hot seat. "Sit down Maggie. Would you like a cup of coffee?" She asked.

Maggie shook her head in the negative. Trembling hands and a cup of hot liquid were a dangerous combination.

Sheila folded her hands on top of her massive oak desk. Was it new, or did it just seem larger? Her gaze locked with Maggie's and her expression softened. Perhaps this wouldn't be so bad after all. "Maggie, let me start by saying that I am concerned about you. Is there anything you would like to talk about? Have you been ill, or is something bothering you? I'd like to help if I can."

Maggie's mouth gaped open. She snapped it shut, hoping Sheila hadn't noticed. This was crazy. Sheila wanted to discuss her health? Was she supposed to break down and confess to some mysterious malady or crisis at home? Suddenly, she felt stronger and more in control of the situation.

"I appreciate your concern." Maggie answered. "But, I'm fine. I would like to apologize one more time for the Jonsgaard fiasco. I was relieved to hear we still won the contract."

Sheila nodded, kindness and compassion gleamed in her eyes. She truly cared about Maggie. "I know you're sorry and I haven't forgotten all the hard work you put into the contract. However, I have to be honest with you. Your work hasn't been up to par lately. You seem distracted and unorganized and frankly, I'm concerned. Are you sure there isn't something you would like to share with me?"

Maggie swallowed hard. Suddenly, she was back on the defensive. Lately she had to explain herself to everyone. Now it seemed

Sheila had joined the club. A single tear slipped down her cheek. "Sheila, please believe me, there is nothing wrong. I haven't been sleeping well lately. I'm a little tired, that's all. I promise I'll do better."

Sheila forced a smile. This was the worst part of being a boss. She hated this type of confrontation, especially with someone like Maggie. She was part of the backbone of the company. Her hard work and dedication, for over twenty years, helped build the business into the success it was today. But it was more than that. Maggie wasn't just an employee, Sheila considered her a friend. Unfortunately, that only made this unpleasant situation more difficult. She didn't have a choice. She had cut Maggie as much slack as she could, and there had been too many complaints to ignore. There was no denying it. The quality of Maggie's work had drastically declined.

Sheila sighed. "I hope things do get better for you Maggie. I sincerely do, and I'll be happy to help you any way I can. However, there have been numerous complaints from several of your coworkers, and I believe they are valid."

Maggie listened in disbelief. Her temper flared. "Who complained about me?" She demanded. Her voice thundered in anger.

Sheila shook her head. "That isn't important. Your health and well-being are what concerns me the most. I want you to take a two week vacation, paid of course, starting immediately. And I think it might be a good idea for you to see a doctor."

Maggie exhaled. It was as if Sheila had kicked her in the stomach. This whole conversation was surreal and beyond her comprehension. Had the entire world gone insane, or was she losing her mind? She struggled to remain calm, while every nerve fiber in her body ached to destroy something. She wanted to hurt someone or something, to cause pain and relish in it. The evil thoughts shocked her. Words escaped her. What could she possibly say? There wasn't a chance in hell she would demean herself by begging for a second chance.

Maggie meekly nodded and stood to leave. She had heard more than enough and she wouldn't sit through another second of this torture. She bit her lower lip until she tasted blood and fought back the flood of tears that threatened to fall.

Sheila stood behind her desk; grateful the ordeal was over. It was a difficult thing to do and her heart was filled with pity and compassion, but she had no choice. It had to be done. She was genuinely concerned about Maggie. There was something amiss. Hopefully, she would follow her advice and seek medical attention. Perhaps there was a logical answer to her problems. But, that was in John's hands now, and she didn't envy him the job. Sheila extended her hand and prayed Maggie would accept this small expression of friendship.

Maggie swallowed her pride and accepted Sheila's hand, if nothing else she would leave with some dignity. She marched past the secretary's desk with her head held high and made it a point to acknowledge everyone she passed on her way to her office. The back stabbing jerks wouldn't get the satisfaction of seeing how deeply hurt she was.

~

Journal Entry

John accepted the news about my mandatory vacation with amazing grace and understanding. He didn't seem surprised by the news at all. It was almost as if he knew about it before I told him. He probably did. He and Sheila are probably in cahoots too.

Well, they can all go to hell. I don't need them. They won't beat me down. If Sheila wants to give me a free two week vacation, I damn well intend to enjoy every minute of it.

Maggie

8

Maggie lingered in bed, pretending to sleep. Let John make his own breakfast for a change. She was on vacation. It was a childish attempt to punish him, but if she was going to be treated like a child, she might as well act like one.

She remained under the covers until she heard John's car pull out of the driveway. The coast was clear. She threw on her favorite ratty old terry cloth robe and pattered into the kitchen for a cup of coffee. There was a note from John laying on the breakfast bar, telling her to enjoy her first day of vacation. Five twenty dollar bills were tucked under it. Wow, her weekly allowance! Not bad, for a sixty-two year old woman. It was just another insult to her already bruised ego.

She poured a tall mug of coffee and wrapped her hands around the mug. Its warmth was comforting and eased the ache in her arthritic fingers. Growing old was sure fun. She glanced around the kitchen, feeling somewhat lost. What in the world was she going to do with herself for two weeks?

The morning sunlight poured through the patio windows and Maggie smiled. What the heck, she might as well indulge herself. Armed with her coffee, the morning paper, and her cigarettes she went out on the patio. She must have looked a sight in her tattered robe and bed head, but she didn't care. Let the neighbors get an eyeful.

There was still a chill in the air, but it promised to be a beautiful day. Morning was her favorite time of day. Another new beginning, she thought and frowned. She lit a cigarette and took a deep drag. Perhaps

Sheila was right. Two weeks away from the stress of the office would do her good. Besides, didn't absence make the heart grow fonder? They would miss her. She would concede that she probably wasn't working up to par, but she still carried her share of the work load. Someone would have to pick it up while she was gone. She smiled at the thought.

She forced the unpleasant thoughts from her mind and gazed at her backyard with a critical eye. They lived in one of the oldest sections of town. Natives referred to it as "below the hog line." Apparently, at one time this was the only section of town where city dwellers were still allowed to raise hogs. Polish immigrants settled here and made the most of the land by building their houses incredibly close together. In some cases, you could literally reach out of a window and touch your neighbor's house. John and Maggie were fortunate to have a double lot. Their backyard was large, but looking at it now, it seemed barren and neglected. The lawn was mowed, but weeds were quickly overtaking the grass. It was a depressing sight.

She smiled. This was a perfect project for her vacation time. It wasn't too late in the season to plant and she had plenty of time on her hands. Suddenly, she was charged with excitement and an energy she hadn't felt in months.

Her feet took on a life of their own. She ran into the house and hastily changed into an old worn out sweatshirt and faded jeans. She was vainly pleased the jeans still fit. Thankfully, she had mercifully been spared the trauma of the middle-aged spread. She might be losing her mind, but she still had the waistline of a woman half her age.

Time was a wasting and she was eager to get to work. First, she had to find her gardening tools. They were buried in a box in the garage, underneath other unused items. They looked so new and shiny, it was embarrassing, but she would soon remedy that. With a little hard work, she would transform her neglected yard into a garden paradise. She could almost taste the barbecues she and John would enjoy, surrounded by lush green grass and the colorful flowers she would plant. John will be so pleased, she thought with a smile.

The weeds would be her first victim. She dug into her project with zeal. It wasn't her favorite job, but it was a necessary evil. It wasn't long before she looked like a piece of the earth herself. Her hips and back ached, dirt and sweat covered her clothes and her face, but she didn't rest until the yard was void of the unwanted invaders.

Time seemed to stop. She heard a car and was shocked to see John pulling into the driveway. Heavens, it was well after five o'clock. A rumble from her tummy reminded her that she hadn't even stopped for lunch, and now she realized with dismay, she hadn't thought to defrost anything for dinner.

John found her in the backyard and approached her with a puzzled look on his face. He paused for a moment and studied her from head to toe, before bursting out in laughter.

"I've been weeding." Maggie explained and giggled.

John scanned the yard and pulled Maggie into his arms. She struggled against him. "Stop it John. I'll get you all dirty."

John only smiled and pulled her closer. A little dirt was the least of his worries. He kissed Maggie's muddied forehead and breathed a sigh of relief. Thank God, she was okay. He had been so worried about her. He tried calling home several times throughout the day, and he became more nervous each time the answering machine picked up. He didn't want to offend Maggie on her first day of vacation by checking on her, but he couldn't argue with his instincts. Maggie had given him good reason to be concerned. It was a relief to find her safe, even though she didn't smell so good.

"Well," John said. "You've certainly have been a busy beaver. And to think I was worried you'd be bored."

Maggie laughed in response. There was no danger of that. She had a garden to grow. They strolled the perimeter of their small piece of land, arm in arm. Maggie proudly pointed out all that she had already accomplished and shared her plans for planting flowers. She was glowing with pride, and John's heart warmed as he became caught up in her excitement. Perhaps, everything would be okay after all.

The second day of vacation began very similar to Maggie's first. She remained in bed while John, once again prepared his own breakfast. However, there wasn't a hidden agenda this time. She had no desire to punish him. The thought of moving made her cringe. Every muscle in her body screamed in protest to the slightest stir, but it was time to rise and shine. She couldn't stay in bed all day. With gritted teeth, she forced her limbs to move.

She dressed in her dirty clothes from the day before and added a baseball cap to her gardening attire. Her nose was already a shiny pink from the sun. A few good stretches loosened up her back and she prayed the pain would ease in time. She poured herself a large mug of coffee and swallowed three aspirins. Armed with her coffee, a spiral notebook and some back issues of a gardening magazine that she had laying around the house for some odd reason, Maggie settled on the patio. There was nary a weed in sight. Satisfied with the results of her labor so far, she decided it was time to move on to more pleasant endeavors. Looking to the magazines for inspiration, she made several rough sketches of their backyard.

Frustrated by her lack of imagination and skill, she decided a trip to the nursery was what she needed to fuel her creativity. Her allowance was more than enough to buy flowers, or at least give her a good start. The yellow pages described the perfect place. This was no ordinary nursery, they also boasted fresh honey from their own bee hives, a bakery and more. The ad promised an answer to all her gardening questions. It sounded like the perfect place for a novice gardener like herself.

The nursery was located outside of town, up on the ridge. Maggie wasn't very familiar with the area, but the ad offered good directions. It shouldn't be too difficult to find.

She drove to the nursery without making a single wrong turn. As it turned out, the nursery was located on a farm. It was definitely a unique operation and she was glad she made the trip. She stepped out of her car and joined the throng of shoppers milling around the flats of flowers spread out in the open-air market. Maggie was shocked by the crowd. Didn't anyone work any more? The abundance of flowers and bright colors exhilarated and confused her. There were petunias, pansies, begonias, and geraniums that she recognized, but there were so many she couldn't begin to put a name to. How could she begin to choose?

A young girl finally approached her and inquired if she needed assistance. Boy, did she ever. With the young girl's patience and guidance, Maggie finally decided on a number of plants as well as two planters for the patio. She loaded her treasures into the trunk and back seat of her car, more than satisfied with her choices.

Visions of her completed project danced in her mind. Her barren backyard was about to be transformed into a paradise of vibrant colors and tranquil greenery. Her gay reverie was abruptly interrupted by the realization that she had been driving far too long.

Her pulse quickened as she pulled over to the shoulder and stopped the car. She seemed to be in the middle of nowhere. Nothing surrounding her was familiar. Damn, how could she be so stupid. She made a U-turn and backtracked. What a waste of time. She struggled to remain calm. Under the best of circumstances, she had a lousy sense of direction. John loved to tease that she was the only person he knew that could get lost going around the block. An absentminded glance at the gas gauge nearly stopped her rapidly beating heart. It was almost on empty. How could that be? She never allowed her tank to go lower than half. The answer was undeniable. She had forgotten ... Again.

She longed for a familiar sight, anything that might help her get her bearings. Even a passing car would be comforting, but the road was empty and there wasn't a house in sight. She drove aimlessly, wasting precious gas. Her heart leaped at the sight of a farm house, but it quickly sank when she passed it and realized it was obviously abandoned. No one could possibly inhabit the sad structure except rats and snakes. She shuddered at the thought.

Frantic with despair, she slammed on the brakes and the car fishtailed slightly before it came to a sudden stop in the middle of the road. There was no need to park properly. She wasn't in any danger of being rear-ended. There hadn't been another car in sight for over an hour. She lit a cigarette to settle her nerves. There was no denying it. She was desperately lost. A search party would eventually find her emaciated body, propped up behind the steering wheel of the car. Her family and Sheila would just nod their heads at the news. Their ugly suspicions about her would be confirmed. She was a senile old woman who couldn't even find her way home.

Disgusted by her own thoughts, she slammed the transmission into drive and thanked God her car was good on gas. A torrent of tears nearly blinded her. She was close to uncontrolled hysterics when she saw the intersection to highway 61 in front of her. Thank God, she was almost home.

She laughed out loud as she pulled into her driveway. Home had never been a more welcome sight. The frightening ordeal, as well as her empty gas tank, was quickly forgotten as she focused all of her attention and energy on her flowers. She worked at a feverish pace until every plant was placed firmly in the ground.

She was filthy, exhausted and famished. In other words, she was damn proud of herself.

9

What a wonderful vacation. I can't remember when I've enjoyed myself more. I suppose I should thank Sheila for insisting on it, but I would never give her the satisfaction. The days are slipping by too quickly, and I must confess there is a part of me that dreads going back to work. I could get used to being a lady of leisure, although I think I've worked harder during this vacation than I ever have sitting behind my desk.

The backyard is almost complete and I couldn't be more pleased with the results. It cost more than I anticipated, but for once John didn't complain about the money. I suppose he thought it was worth the price to keep me busy and out of trouble.

I have made one concession in my plans. I've made it a point to stick closer to home. Thank goodness there is a nursery just a few blocks from here. I didn't tell John about my little adventure. It was too embarrassing, and it's probably better he doesn't know. I guess things are better between us, but our communication is still strained. I miss the way it used to be. It used to be so easy to talk to John. I could tell him anything without worrying about his response. Now, I find myself keeping more and more secrets from him. He hovers over me and monitors my every move, and overreacts to everything I say or do. If he knew I got lost, he would probably take my car keys away. So, the way I figure it, what he doesn't know, won't hurt me.

Thankfully, he does seem pleased with my gardening project, although he doesn't share my enthusiasm. He seems so distant. What can I do to make things right again?

Maggie

~

Journal Entry

I've screwed up again! It seems no matter how hard I try, I just can't seem to do anything right. John is angry at me. We had a terrible fight this morning. I'm still shaking from the intensity of it. We rarely fought before, but now we can't seem to agree on anything.

I'll admit that I've been preoccupied with my project, and I've probably neglected the housework, but I thought I was supposed to be on vacation. John isn't helpless, he knows where the laundry room is and it doesn't take a rocket scientist to operate a washing machine. At the very least, he could have told me he was running low on dress shirts. And I'll admit, I haven't been cooking any gourmet meals, or any kind of meal for that matter, but neither one of us look like we are in any danger of blowing away in a breeze. At any rate, I didn't expect him to go crazy about it. He totally lost control.

Everyone is so damned worried about me, but I'm beginning to wonder if their concern is misplaced. Perhaps it is John they should be worried about? He seems so unhappy lately and little things seem to upset him. Perhaps he is having problems at work. If I had a more suspicious nature, I might wonder if he was involved with another woman. That would explain his constant criticism of everything I do.

But, I know better, don't I? Dear God, perhaps I don't measure up to my competition.

No, I won't allow myself to consider it. I've never had reason to question John's fidelity before, and I refuse to start now. Those kind of doubts can destroy a relationship and we're on tenuous ground now. But, I wonder...

It's another beautiful day, but I better force myself to stay inside and catch up with some "women's work". I hate quarreling with John. Maggie

~

Journal Entry

Katie paid me a surprise visit this morning. I love her dearly, but a phone call before dropping by would have been nice. She caught me in the backyard, planting hostas by the garage. I realize I was a dirty mess, but I wasn't expecting company. She looked at me as if I'd lost my mind. I was having a wonderful time before she arrived. She made me feel foolish and I found myself trying to defend myself. Again.

I excused myself and washed up. I played hostess well enough to bring some lemonade and cookies (store bought of course) out to the patio. There is no denying I was irritated by the interruption, but I was determined to have a pleasant visit with my daughter. Boy, was I in for a shock. Katie seemed to have a different agenda. It was more like an inquisition than a visit. She grilled me like a police detective interrogating a criminal. Why must I defend everything I do?

One would think everyone would be happy that I found something constructive to do with my free time. Instead, the general consensus seems to be that I've gone off the deep end. Katie's endless questions made me so mad, I couldn't control myself. Our visit quickly escalated into a screaming match. We both said some terribly hurtful things. And to think it all started because I decided to plant a few flowers. You would think I was assembling nuclear bombs in the backyard.

I feel as though I have been dropped from the sky into the Twilight Zone. What has happened to my life and my family? According to Katie, John thinks I am acting strangely and wants me to see a doctor, and she agrees. Why is everyone turning against me? I've devoted my life to loving and caring for them. Why are they betraying me now?

Perhaps I'm just outgrowing my usefulness. Or maybe my suspicions are valid and John is planning on replacing me with a new model. Has he met someone younger and more capable than me?

I vow to God in heaven. I will not give up my husband and family without a fight!
Maggie

~

Journal Entry

I can't sit still. My nerve endings feel like they are on fire. This is the eve of the end of my vacation. Tomorrow, I will have to discard the comfort of my blue jeans in exchange for grown-up clothes. It's almost worse than the first day of school.

The only good thing I can say about it is that John has been kinder and more sympathetic to my feelings. To his credit, he hasn't mentioned my argument with Katie, although I'm sure he has heard about it. Those two are thick as thieves these days. He keeps asking me if I'm sure I'm ready to return to work. I don't know what difference that makes, I wasn't aware I had a choice. This was just a vacation, not retirement.

Well, it's been fun while it lasted. And I did manage to accomplish something constructive during my time off. The backyard looks great!

It will probably be good to get back to work...

Maggie

10

"Maggie, are you sure you're ready for this? You look absolutely green." John asked, as he discreetly studied her from across the kitchen table. Dark shadows rimmed her eyes and her complexion was a lighter shade of pale. If the constant tossing and turning in bed was any indication, John was certain she had barely slept all night. He certainly hadn't.

Maggie shook her head and took a sip of hot black coffee. She felt horrible and her stomach reacted violently. It was a fight to keep the liquid down. She hated to waste the lovely breakfast John prepared for her, and she certainly didn't want to hurt his feelings, but she had no choice. She pushed the plate of scrambled eggs and bacon away. "I'm sorry honey. I don't know why I'm so nervous. I've only been gone for two weeks."

It broke John's heart to see her so distraught. "I'd be happy to call Sheila and ask for an extension of your time off. I'm sure it wouldn't be a problem. Another week off would probably do you good."

Anger flashed in Maggie's eyes. "How can you be so sure she would agree? Do you know something I don't?"

"No." He paused for just a moment. "Of course not, but knowing Sheila, and given the circumstances..."

Maggie slowly and deliberately rose to her feet and braced her hands on the table. Fire danced in her eyes. "Circumstances?"

She questioned. "And just what circumstances are you referring to? Are you afraid to let your nut case of a wife back out into the public eye and out of your sight? Well, let me tell you something mister. I am sick to tears of you, Katie, Sheila and everyone else treating me like a feeble-minded old woman. I accepted Sheila's discipline because she is my employer. That doesn't mean I agree with her. But you..." She pointed an accusing finger at John. "You are my husband, not my boss. You can't tell me what to do. Now, if you'll excuse me, I'm going to work." She grabbed her purse and stormed out of the door.

Suddenly, all of her doubts and fears evaporated. Anger fueled her courage and sustained her until she settled into the familiar comfort of her office chair. She straightened her desk and checked her priority file. After a two week absence, she was prepared to be overwhelmed. She was shocked to find the file nearly empty. There were only a few slips of paper tucked inside. They were insignificant items that normally would be handled by the receptionist. Puzzled by this discovery, she opened her file drawer and was shocked to find it nearly empty. Of course, someone would have had to cover for her during her vacation, but she didn't expect to find her office stripped.

Maggie leaned back in her chair and sighed. Was this a hint of things to come? Apparently twenty years of loyal service didn't count for much, here or at home. She wasn't going to take this laying down. She refused to be a token employee, a paper pusher. With twenty years of experience, she had too much to offer. Sheila deserved the benefit of the doubt. There had to be a logical explanation for this. Perhaps she planned to ease her back into a full work load, but Maggie knew better. The empty file drawer told the tale.

It took less than fifteen minutes to handle the few items in the priority file. Left with nothing to do, Maggie found the silence of the office unnerving. She drummed the desktop with her fingertips, and stared at the phone, willing it to ring. It suddenly dawned on her that she hadn't seen anyone since she came in. She hadn't expected a welcome back party, but certainly someone should have stopped in to say hello by now. Was she being ignored, like some kind of a leper?

Anger grew like a fire in her belly. There was only one thing to do. She had to confront the problem head on. They wouldn't put her out to pasture without a fight. Determined to speak her mind, she marched to Sheila's office and ignored the secretary poised to stop her. She rapped loudly on the door, and without waiting for a response, stepped inside.

Sheila propped her reading glasses on top of her head and motioned Maggie to come in. "Good morning Maggie. Welcome back. I wanted to give you some time to settle in before I came to see you. Would you like to join me for lunch today?"

Maggie stepped forward. "I'm really not hungry, but I would like an explanation."

Sheila raised a perfectly arched eyebrow in surprise. She was expecting this conversation, just not so soon. "Maggie, sit down and let's talk about this."

Maggie took a deep breath and sat. Keep calm, she told herself. Sheila was fair. Give her a chance to explain. "I had a few surprises waiting for me this morning. I realize someone had to cover for me during my so called vacation, but I didn't expect to find my office ransacked and stripped. And what was that crap in my priority file? I want to know what the hell is going on."

Sheila nervously cleared her throat and folded her hands. "Well Maggie, to be honest, that is exactly what I wanted to discuss with you over lunch. There were some changes made while you were gone. You might call it a restructuring of sorts. I want you to understand, this was a simple business decision. It was nothing personal."

"And was anyone else affected by this business decision, or was it just me?"

Sheila visibly squirmed in her seat. The hot seat wasn't a comfortable chair. "No, of course not. I'm afraid this is just an unfortunate sign of the times. We aren't the first company forced to cut back and I'm sure we won't be the last. With the economy being what it is, it's simply a matter of survival."

"Cut backs, are you trying to tell me I'm fired?" Maggie asked, fear gleaming in her eyes.

"No, certainly not." Sheila answered, quick to reassure. "You are a valuable employee. I just want to change the focus of your position in the company. My plan is to utilize your knowledge and experience by making you a mentor of sorts to the younger associates. I think you will enjoy the opportunity. Besides, it will lighten your workload considerably. As a matter of fact, you should be able to cut back your work week by almost twenty hours. Of course, that won't affect your benefit package."

Maggie shook her head in disbelief and chuckled. She recognized a snow job when she heard one. Sheila was trying to force her into retirement. It was the straw that broke the camel's back. Her stomach churned as her body flushed with an unbearable heat. Something inside of her snapped. Suddenly, the world narrowed to a small tunnel, where only she and Sheila existed. She stood and took a step toward Sheila's desk. Her legs felt like lead and she seemed to be moving in slow motion. A shrill scream pierced the air and Maggie was shocked to realize the sound emanated from her own mouth.

"You can't do this to me!" Maggie shouted. "There are laws against this. I'll sue, you bastard."

Sheila's mouth gaped open in shock and fear. This wasn't the same gentle woman she had known for nearly a quarter of a century. Maggie wasn't just angry; she was out of control. Fear gripped her as she fought the urge to escape. It was imperative that she remain calm and in control of this volatile situation. "Maggie, please calm down. Let's talk about this." She pleaded.

But it was an impossible request. Maggie's mind and body had taken on a frenzied momentum beyond her control. Her fist slammed Sheila's desk. And with one deliberate sweep of her arm, she sent everything on the oak desktop crashing to the floor.

Maggie turned on her heels and stormed to the door. She paused and turned. The expression on her face was venomous and the look raised the hair on Sheila's neck. "Fuck you!" The unfamiliar word flowed from her lips as naturally as a drunken sailor's. A one-fingered salute accentuated the phrase as she walked out the door, nearly knocking a shocked Doris off her feet.

11

Is it possible that it has only been two days since my world ended? It seems like a distant dream that fades in and out of focus. There are times I can almost convince myself that it was a dream, but then, reality grips me and my stomach ties itself into knots.

I have no recollection of leaving my office or the drive home, but I'll never forget the sight of John waiting at the kitchen table with his head buried in his hands. The image will haunt my memory forever. I walked into the room and he slowly raised his face to look at me. Tear tracks stained his face. As upset as I was, his anguish stopped me short. My problems at work were instantly forgotten, replaced with a sickening fear. I was certain a terrible tragedy had befallen us. Fear for my family gripped me. My knees buckled and I collapsed into the chair next to him, bracing myself to hear the terrible news.

I waited for an eternity, barely able to breathe and silently begging John to speak, yet not wanting to hear the words. He simply stared at me. I wanted to physically shake him and force the words out of his mouth. The stillness was driving me to the brink of madness.

Finally, he shook his head, almost as if he were clearing cobwebs from his mind. In a shaky, gravelly voice, he told me that Sheila had called him at the bank. Relief washed over me and I offered a silent prayer to God for keeping my family safe. I was so grateful, I barely heard John's words has he recounted his conversation with Sheila.

As soon as his words registered in my still numb mind, I interrupted and launched into an animated version of my side of the story. I rambled for several minutes, explaining my grandiose plans of hiring an attorney and suing the pants off Sheila and her company. I was so engaged by the sound of my own voice, it took me several minutes to realize John didn't seem to share my zeal for justice.

John reached for my hand and held it tenderly in his. Speaking slowly and deliberately, as if it were rehearsed, he confirmed my conspiracy theory. It seems he and my dear friend Sheila have spoken frequently during the past months. John knew about my two week vacation before I did. As a matter of fact, he was the one who originally suggested it. He told me he loved me and was worried about me. He cried like a baby as he spoke his hurtful words.

I listened in stunned silence. Words can't describe the devastation his confession inflicted upon me. It was beyond my comprehension. My husband, the same man who stood before God, and promised to stand by my side until death do us part, had betrayed me.

I was speechless and I felt so cold, so very cold. Tears flooded my eyes and for once, I made no effort to stop them. I embraced the sobs that wracked my body as my due. I was alone, with no one to turn to for comfort or solace.

John tried to reach out to me, but I pulled away. His touch sickened me. As far as I was concerned, he was now the enemy. I turned a deaf ear while he pleaded for my understanding. He begged me to talk to him, but I had no voice, there were no words to say. He fell to his knees and buried his tear stained face in my lap. We didn't move. We were frozen in time, each of us lost in our separate universe of fear.

Maggie

~

Journal Entry

I'm going to the doctor. It's a waste of time, but I'll go to ease John's mind (and to prove him wrong). I hate to see him so worried and upset, although his concern still baffles and angers me. I am trying to keep my cool about it. It wouldn't be wise to add any more fuel to John's fire. After all, just because I'm paranoid, doesn't mean they aren't out to get me. I can't afford any more outbursts like the one in Sheila's office.

John even went so far as to call a family meeting to discuss my "problems". The kangaroo court met in our living room. Even Michael was in attendance. It was an indescribable experience. I felt as though I was on trial for my life, with my husband and family serving as both my judge and my jury.

Michael was the worst. He watched my every move, and seemed to examine me with his "doctor's eyes". Katie was the complete opposite. She didn't even have the pluck to look me in the eye. Poor Craig sat in the corner, looking lost and as if he would give a million dollars to be anywhere else in the world than in that room. I was on his team.

I sat back and let everyone else do the talking. I made no attempt to defend myself. It would have been a waste of my time and breath. I was outnumbered, and the verdict in my case had been decided before the court was called to order.

I won't deny that the prospect of a doctor's visit makes me slightly nervous, but I stand firm in my belief that there is nothing wrong with me. I'm just not crazy about doctors, excluding my son of course, although he's not exactly at the top of my list at the moment.

I'll concede that I have been a tad bit forgetful lately, but certainly nothing so serious to warrant all of this hoopla and concern. After all, forgetting a few things, getting lost and acting crazy doesn't mean you are sick, does it?

John is planning on going to my appointment with me. It's just one more slap in the face and another example of his lack of trust in me. Isn't it enough that I've agreed to go? I'm not a child that needs to be supervised. I'm fully capable of going to the doctor by myself. Although, as I think about it, it may not be such a bad idea to have John with me. I can't wait to see the expression on his face when Dr. Hardy declares me fit as a fiddle and sound of mind.

I promise not to be too smug about it, but it will be a tremendous pleasure to tell him, "I told you so."
Maggie

12

Maggie stared at the clock in the doctor's waiting room. Were the hands moving at all? Her appointment wasn't until nine, but of course John insisted on being early. In Maggie's estimation, the only thing worse than a doctor's examination, was the waiting room. She picked up a dog eared magazine and absentmindedly flipped through its worn pages. Finding nothing that held her interest, she tossed it back onto the table.

An elderly woman, smiled at Maggie and unceremoniously coughed in her face, while a young mother sitting across from her, wiped her child's nose. Maggie shuddered. If you have a desire to get sick, just hang out in a doctor's office for a while. She almost giggled as she considered the possibility of hanging a sign ... WARNING: DOCTOR'S WAITING ROOMS CAN BE HAZARDOUS TO YOUR HEALTH!

A nurse stepped into the waiting room. Maggie held her breath. It was almost like being on a game show. Who would be the next contestant on the "what is your diagnosis" game? Maggie's name was called. Suddenly, she didn't feel like a winner. This was it, the moment of truth. She stood to follow the nurse and felt John's shadow behind her. She turned and glared at him with exasperation. Apparently, she wasn't even allowed the dignity of going into the examination room alone.

Before she had the chance to give John a piece of her mind, Dr. Hardy bounced into the room. He was a large man, the victim of too many meals on the run and the beneficiary of cookies and cakes from grateful patients. He was a rumpled mess. His lab coat was wrinkled and a stubble of whiskers peppered his face. In all likelihood, he had probably spent most of the night at the hospital, delivering a baby or watching over a critically ill patient. But, he seemed to possess an endless supply of energy. Maggie couldn't recall a time he appeared tired or worn out. He had been their family doctor for years, and a mentor of sorts to Michael.

John and Dr. Hardy exchanged a friendly handshake. "Good morning folks, what can I do for you today?" Dr. Hardy asked as he unceremoniously plopped down in a chair with Maggie's medical chart perched on his lap.

Maggie swallowed back the lump in her throat. "To be honest ..." She started. "I'm not sure there is anything you can do for us. I'm not even sure why we are bothering you with this. But," She threw up her hands in mock surrender. "I was outvoted, so here we are."

John vociferously cleared his throat, making it clear that he was taking over the interview. "It isn't quite that simple Dr. Hardy. Maggie has been experiencing some problems with her memory. In the beginning, the change was quite subtle and I wasn't overly concerned, but it seems to be getting worse."

Maggie gritted her teeth and listened as John recited an alarming description of every mishap and mistake she had experienced in the past several months. Had he been taking notes? But, he was telling the truth. She couldn't dispute a word he said. However, to hear the stories spoken out loud, made it seem much worse than it really was.

She listened in disbelief and mounting anger. She struggled to remain calm. It would only strengthen John's case against her if she succumbed to her instincts and ran screaming from the room. They would definitely declare her insane.

She listened in silence until it was impossible to hold her tongue a second longer. "Okay," she abruptly interrupted and shot John a menacing glare. "I'll admit that I've been a bit forgetful lately, but my God, he is making it sound like I've become a blubbering idiot. So, I'm not as young as I used to be, and I've made a few mistakes. I've never claimed to be perfect, but that doesn't mean I need a doctor. As far as I'm concerned, this is a total waste of time and money."

Dr. Hardy didn't respond, he simply listened and observed. Occasionally, he would scribble a few words in Maggie's chart, but his expression remained placid. It was impossible to guess what, if anything, he thought of John and Maggie's stressed interaction. Maggie decided he would make a great card player, he certainly had the poker face for it.

Dr. Hardy laid the metal chart on the desk, leaned slightly forward and folded his hands over his knees. "Well, let's start with the obvious. Maggie, I have known you and John for too many years to count, and to be honest, what John has told me is disturbing. It certainly sounds out of character for you. You obviously don't agree with his observations, but I think it would be a good idea to investigate a little further."

He extended his hand and stopped Maggie short. "Now, before you get all defensive, I want to make it perfectly clear that forgetfulness isn't an inevitable part of aging. However, there are numerous medical conditions that can produce dementia like symptoms."

Maggie winced at the word dementia. It had an ugly sound and she didn't appreciate it being applied to her.

Dr. Hardy noticed Maggie's apprehension and was quick to reassure her. "Maggie, the majority of these conditions are very treatable. Let's see what we are dealing with before you get too worried or upset. Now, I would normally have my nurse draw a blood sample, but I really need the practice ... So, if you don't mind..." He picked up a syringe and held it in exaggerated trembling hands.

Maggie laughed in spite of her fear and anger at John. "I think I would prefer to have you practice on another patient." She answered.

"Very well, if you insist." He chuckled. "But I want you to know that you've hurt my feelings." He smiled warmly and placed a gentle hand on Maggie's shoulder. "I want to run a complete blood test. We'll be checking for any sign of anemia, infections, diabetes and kidney or liver disease. We'll also check your vitamin B12 and folic acid levels. It's a good beginning and hopefully we'll know more when the test results come back. I'll send a nurse in to take the blood sample. I also want a urine sample. After that, you're free to go home. We'll call you when we have the results. In the meantime, get plenty of rest and don't worry."

John and Maggie left the doctor's office in subdued silence. There were too many unanswered questions. Maggie still didn't have the opportunity to say "I told you so", and as easy going as Dr. Hardy was, there was something disconcerting about the way a doctor talks. It made her nervous. Not to mention, she was mad as hell at John for the terrible things he said about her. She had to admit, there was a ring of truth in everything he said, but he certainly exaggerated to make his point.

13

John and I haven't talked about our visit to Dr. Hardy, but then again, we haven't really talked about anything. I guess we've come to a relatively amicable truce, with an unspoken agreement that the subject is taboo. Nonetheless, it weighs heavy on my heart and mind.

Waiting for the test results is pure torture. It's driving me crazy (OOOPS, poor choice of words). Every time the phone rings, my heart skips a beat. I don't expect bad news, but I'm trying to prepare myself for the worst.

Maggie

~

Journal Entry

The phone call finally came while John was at work today. I could hardly breathe while Dr. Hardy's nurse reported the results to me. Good news! Everything came back normal! My feet nearly left the floor in celebration. There was nothing wrong with me. I felt vindicated and we could finally put this nonsense behind us.

Unfortunately, my revelry was short lived. Apparently Dr. Hardy didn't share my positive prognosis. He wants John and I to return to his office tomorrow for another appointment. The nurse asked if that would be convenient for us. Not hardly, but we will be there.

Maggie

~

<u>*Journal Entry*</u>

Thank God, we're finally back home. What a horrible day. My mind is numb and my body aches as though I've just completed a marathon, and believe me, I'm no athlete.

I'm not blind. I noticed a marked difference in Dr. Hardy's demeanor during this visit. There weren't any sappy jokes or friendly chitchat. He was all doctor with a capital D. He sat down and got straight to the point. My mind raced as I tried to concentrate on his words. He started out by repeating what the nurse had told me on the telephone. My blood test showed no indication of any of the conditions he tested for, nor could he see any outward signs of heart or lung disease. However, he did take advantage of that moment to encourage me to quit smoking. Little did he know, I would have killed for a cigarette at that moment.

I listened intently. I didn't want to miss a thing. Everything he had to say seemed like good news to me, yet it was apparent by the expression on his face, he didn't share my positive outlook.

Dr. Hardy's expression softened. He leaned forward and took my hand in his. He spoke clearly and compassionately, almost as if he were speaking to a child. He told me that although the tests came back negative, he was still troubled by the things John told him during our last visit. He wanted to refer us to a neurologist for further testing.

My heart thumped uncontrollably. Surely this was a symptom of the heart condition Dr. Hardy mentioned earlier. I welcomed that possibility. It had to be better than the suspicion he was keeping secret. A referral to a neurologist sounded serious, and ominous. Dr. Hardy wouldn't suggest it unless he felt it was necessary, but that knowledge only increased my fear. What did he suspect? What was he looking for? I had a million questions spinning through my mind, but I couldn't summon the courage to ask one. I didn't want the answers.

I turned to John, praying for a reassuring smile, a touch of his hand, perhaps a glimmer of hope. Instead, he seemed to be a million miles away. His complexion had turned ashen gray. His eyes were focused on the floor. He never looked at me and he never said a word. Why has he abandoned me?

I will be strong. I will do everything the good doctor asks of me, but I stand firm in my belief that there is nothing wrong with me... Maggie

~

Journal Entry

My appointment with the neurologist is scheduled for two weeks from today. The doctor's name is Mason. Dr. Hardy tells me he is one of the best in his field. I wonder if that was meant to reassure me? It didn't. It just makes me wonder why I need the best.

I'm torn with mixed emotions. On one hand, the anticipation is driving me crazy. I can hardly wait to get this over with. Yet, on the other hand, I would gladly postpone the appointment indefinitely.

This is too difficult to comprehend. My entire world has changed dramatically. In the blink of an eye, everything familiar and comforting has been torn from me. Perhaps I'm being punished for taking the simple, worry free days of my past life for granted. Oh, how I long for those days now. I feel like a stranger in my own home, and my own body.

John and I go through the motions of daily life. We perform our mundane chores like robots and stare at the television like zombies. We don't talk to each other. We tiptoe around each other. I'm sure John is as preoccupied with his own thoughts and fears as I am, but why can't we share them with each other?

It would be easier if I still had my job to occupy my mind and time. I miss the structure of my "old life". I always knew what I had to do and when I had to do it. Now, I have too much time on my hands, with very little to do. I have completed every put off until tomorrow project at home. The house has never been so clean, but that offers little satisfaction. How many closets can you clean and still remain sane? Besides, I have never aspired to be Martha Stewart. I still have my flowers, but they don't require much care, and to be honest, they have lost much of their appeal.

Perhaps I'm not as strong as I used to be, or want to be. But who could blame me? When I was younger, this would have been a walk in the park, but then again, if I were younger, I probably wouldn't be having this problem. Growing old isn't all it's cracked up to be...

Dear God, I know I don't talk to you often, and I realize I'm not in a position to ask for special favors, but if you could find it in your heart to give me the strength to survive the next two weeks, I would sure appreciate it.

Maggie

14

Maggie watched herself walk into the grocery store on the security monitor. She looked like a wild woman. Did she comb her hair today? Oh well, this was going to be a quick shopping trip and hopefully she wouldn't run into anyone she knew. She strolled the aisles of the store and cursed herself for not bringing a shopping list. A glimpse into her empty refrigerator and bare cupboards prompted this unplanned visit to the store, but now she regretted the decision.

She paused in the canned vegetable section and stared at the seemingly endless supply of peas, corn, beans and some vegetables she'd never heard of. The choices were overwhelming. She picked up a can of mushrooms and stared at the label. Did she need mushrooms? Was this the brand she normally bought? Suddenly, a woman crashed into her cart and rudely reached in front of her. The woman hastily grabbed can after can of vegetables, without giving it a second thought. Maggie flushed with embarrassment. She carefully placed the single can of mushrooms in her cart and slowly moved on down the aisle.

She zigzagged down three aisles and decided she really didn't need mushrooms after all. She turned her cart around, but realized she didn't remember which aisle they came from. How could that be? She had shopped in this store for years and knew it like the back of her hand, or the hair on her head, which wasn't looking very good at the moment either. It was a triumphant moment when she finally found the correct aisle and replaced her can in the appropriate spot. However, the celebration was short-lived. Maggie glanced at her watch and was shocked to discover she had been in the store for over an hour and hadn't decided on a single purchase.

A young store clerk noticed Maggie's distress and took a break from stocking the shelves. He walked over to Maggie. "May I help you with something?" He cautiously asked.

Maggie's mouth gaped open as she stared at the young man as if he were a creature from outer space. Her mind froze and her tongue was tied. Yes, she needed help. She needed a lot of help, but there wasn't anything the store clerk could do for her.

Suddenly, everything seemed to close in on her. Her chest tightened and she couldn't breathe. Without warning, tears filled her eyes and she burst into uncontrollable sobs. She abandoned her cart in the middle of the aisle and ran to the exit as if her life depended on it.

She felt the curious stares of other shoppers as she jogged across the parking lot. She must have looked like a crazed lunatic and she had probably scarred that poor clerk for life, but she couldn't help herself. She had to escape, but to where? Her jog slowed to a walk as she fought to catch her breath. Where was her car? Did she drive her car, or John's? She wandered the parking lot, whimpering like a lost puppy.

Finally, her trusty old blue sedan seemed to appear out of nowhere. She climbed into the driver's seat with relief. Her fear and desperation dissolved into humiliation, and she buried her face into her hands. How could she ever show her face in that store again? Hopefully, there wasn't anyone inside who knew her. The last thing she needed was for John to hear about this.

She had another secret to keep. They were really adding up.

15

The forty-five mile trip to Rochester might has well have been four hundred. Minutes ticked by like hours, and the silence in the car was as oppressing as a tomb. Several futile attempts at small talk were quickly abandoned in favor of their individual solitude.

Dr. Mason's office was located in the renowned Mayo Clinic. US Presidents, celebrities and dignitaries from all over the world went there for their health care. It was the best of the best. Because of that, Maggie and John weren't surprised to find themselves sharing the neurology waiting room with two sheiks and several obviously wealthy patients.

Maggie straightened her blouse in dismay. Apparently one dressed accordingly when you met with Dr. Mason. Unfortunately, no one sent her the memo. She felt old and frumpy and squirmed nervously in her chair.

John gently squeezed her hand. "Don't worry, everything will be okay." He whispered.

Maggie nodded and wished she could believe him, but she couldn't. Santa Claus had ceased to exist in her life a long time ago. The wait seemed endless, and her tension increased by the minute.

Maggie's name was finally called. The nurse ushered Maggie and John into an office. "Please, make yourselves comfortable. Dr. Mason will be with you shortly."

Maggie noticed a framed photograph perched on the corner of the desk. She took a peek and assumed it was a picture of Dr. Mason and his family. The photo was taken outdoors, perhaps during a family barbecue. They looked like a happy bunch. The good doctor appeared to be in his late forties, although she couldn't be sure. She was a terrible judge of age. At any rate, he had a handsome face and a warm smile. The touch of gray at his temples gave him an air of authority. His wife was very attractive, in an unpretentious way. She looked like a nice person, a good friend and neighbor. His three sons were all handsome boys. A perfect family, she thought, and a twinge of envy pinched her heart. She used to believe she had the perfect family. That is, until they all turned against her.

The office door opened and the man in the photograph strolled into the room. John and Maggie instinctively stood to greet him.

"Hello." Dr. Mason said, extending his hand to John. "I'm sorry to keep you waiting so long. It has been a hectic morning, but then again, they are all hectic."

"No problem." John assured him.

Dr. Mason smiled. He settled himself behind his massive desk, opened a file folder and quickly reviewed its contents. After a moment, he turned his attention back to Maggie and John. Maggie's stomach fluttered in anticipation.

"I've reviewed your medical records and Dr. Hardy's notes from your past two visits with him. Apparently there is some concern related to Maggie's memory?"

"Yes." John answered, a little too quickly in Maggie's opinion.

Dr. Mason nodded. "I would like to begin our visit today with a simple mental status exam. This test is a tool used to evaluate memory loss or abnormal thinking processes."

Maggie swallowed. She had never been very good at taking tests of any kind, and she had a feeling this might be the most important test score of her life.

Dr. Mason smiled. "Don't worry Maggie. This isn't nearly as ominous as it sounds. Just relax and answer the questions the best you can."

The test began with some very basic questions. What is the date today? What day of the week is it? What season is it? Maggie answered with ease and began to relax. Perhaps this wouldn't be so bad after all.

The questions continued. What was the name of this medical center? What floor are we on? Maggie struggled with that one, but she recouped with the city and state questions. Hooray!

"Okay Maggie, this is a simple memory test. I am going to say three words. After I've said all three, I want you to repeat them. Are you ready?"

Maggie nodded. This should be a piece of cake. She concentrated on Dr. Mason's lips as she listened to the words.

"Ball ... Flag ... Tree."

Maggie took a deep breath. "Ball ... Flag ..." Her mind went blank. She turned to John, begging for a clue, but he ignored her silent plea. She strained to remember, and started once again. "Ball ... Flag..." Please, let me remember, she prayed. "Tree!" She exclaimed triumphantly.

Her exultation was short-lived. She wasn't able to count backward from one hundred by seven; although she quickly defended herself by explaining math had never been her strong suit. She spelled WORLD backwards with ease and an iota of confidence returned.

"Okay Maggie, I want you to repeat the same three words I recited to you earlier."

Maggie's heart leaped. This was a zinger she hadn't expected. It wasn't fair. Dr. Mason never warned her this might come back to haunt her. It was only three little words. Surely, she could remember, but she couldn't. Finally, she whispered, "Ball", ashamed it was the only word she could recall.

"Don't dwell on it Maggie. It's only one question." Dr. Said, doing his best to reassure her.

She fumbled through the rest of the test, her failure heavy on her mind. What kind of idiot was she that she couldn't remember three stupid words? But, she carried on. She followed the doctor's instructions. She wrote a sentence, drew some pictures and nearly died with relief when Dr. Mason announced the test was complete.

Dr. Mason turned his attention to John. For once, Maggie didn't mind. It was good to be out of the hot seat. At least until she heard the questions he was asking. Did she have any difficulty performing daily tasks, such as managing a checkbook? Maggie cringed as she listened to John repeat the same exaggerated stories he told Dr. Hardy.

Dr. Mason listened with intense interest, taking notes as John spoke. Eventually, John ran out of damning anecdotes about her and silence crushed the room.

Dr. Mason put his pen down and pushed his glasses to the top of his head. "As I explained earlier, the test you just completed is a tool used to detect decrease in cognition and memory. As you may have noticed, they are very broad questions, so your age, past occupation and education are all taken into account during the evaluation process. I realize it must have been difficult for you to listen to the things John had to say, but it is important for me to get a clear picture of your day to day functioning. A close family member is usually the best source for that information. So, please don't be angry with him."

"Now, based on this information, as well as Dr. Hardy's assessment, I have to conclude that there seems to be a significant decrease in Maggie's level of cognition. There are a variety of different causes for this. We just need to pinpoint it."

"I am going to schedule Maggie for a CT scan. That is a procedure where multiple x-rays are taken of the body, from all different angles. Those images are then transferred to a computer that creates images that look like we have actually sliced through the body. With this test, we should be able to rule out the possibility of a brain tumor, a past CVA or blood clots on the brain."

"I am also going to schedule you far an EEG. That is short for electroencephalogram." He smiled. "I know, it's quite a mouthful, but it isn't as bad as it sounds. The test measures brain function by analyzing the electrical activity generated by the brain. This test is useful in identifying many disorders of the brain, epilepsy for example."

The room seemed to be spinning, and for a brief moment, Maggie feared she might faint. Suddenly, the doctor seemed to be speaking a foreign language. She hoped John understood what Dr. Mason was saying. It was all Greek to her.

16

Journal Entry

I thought the tests were dreadful. They were obviously designed by someone who was in command of a torture chamber during a past life. Well, that may be a bit of an exaggeration, but I certainly didn't enjoy myself. The CT scan was hair-raising. I didn't realize I was claustrophobic. The EEG wasn't as scary as it was uncomfortable. I will probably be picking glue out of my head for months.

I am glad that ordeal is over, but now the hard part begins, waiting for the results.

Maggie

~

John and Maggie sat quietly and watched Dr. Mason shuffle through the ever increasing number of pages in Maggie's medical file. Maggie didn't want to hear what Dr. Mason had to say. She couldn't endure any more questions or silly tests. It would be so easy to walk out the door and forget any of this ever happened. That's what she did best wasn't it, forget? She was becoming an expert at denial. But, she forced herself to remain seated.

"Well," Dr. Mason began. "I have carefully reviewed all of your test results. There are several conditions we can completely rule out. Maggie, you do not have Parkinson's or Huntington's disease. There is no evidence of a CVA or epilepsy, and your lab results came back normal."

Maggie's spirit soared. This was finally the good news she had been waiting for. She was prepared to thank Dr. Mason for his time and make a hasty exit. She glanced at John and Dr. Mason and realized she was the only person smiling. Apparently there was more to come. There always was.

Dr. Mason removed his glasses and folded his hands. His expression was solemn. John reached for her hand and she gratefully accepted.

"Medicine is not a perfect science. We have come a long way with research, but we still have a long way to go." He paused and sighed deeply. "There is no easy way to say this, but by the process of elimination, and taking into consideration Maggie's symptoms and mental status test results, I have to conclude probable Alzheimer's Disease."

Maggie's stomach lurched. The "A" word. Why didn't the word shock her? Was this what she had feared all along? "You said probable. Does that mean you aren't sure?" Maggie asked, grasping for a glimmer of hope.

Dr. Mason smiled sympathetically. This was the hardest part of his job. He laid his hands out on the desk. "I am only human, so of course there is always that possibility. However, I said probable because there is no definitive way to diagnose Alzheimer's until after death by autopsy. However, given your symptoms and my many years of experience in this field, I can make this diagnosis with ninety percent accuracy. Of course, you are welcome to get a second opinion, and I would encourage you to do so if you have doubts."

Maggie listened in disbelief. President Reagan was diagnosed with Alzheimer's after he left office and had since passed away. She recalled watching the news reports and thinking how sad it was, but that was distant. It didn't affect her, it was just a woeful story. Now, it was touching her life, and her family. Suddenly, she was hearing words like death and autopsy. She turned to John, praying there had been a mistake. Perhaps she had heard wrong or didn't understand what Dr. Mason was saying.

But, one look at John's ashen face told her it was true. He looked as if he had aged thirty years in the past thirty seconds. In an instant, he was transformed into an old man. He was bent over in his chair, tears streaming down his face. Maggie watched him in silent horror as he seemed to crumble before her eyes, and her fear escalated. John was her strength, her rock. How could she endure this without his solid support?

The room was silent. After a few minutes, John straightened his back, gulped back a sob and wiped his tears away with the back of his hand. "I'm sorry." He apologized. "I don't normally lose control like that."

"Don't worry about it." Dr. Mason reassured him. "You are certainly entitled. I've just dropped quite a bomb on you, and I won't lie to you. There is no cure for Alzheimer's Disease. It is a progressive disease with devastating consequences. However, I would say that Maggie is still in the early stage. In most cases, symptoms progress slowly, over a period of years. So, let's take this one step at a time."

"I am going to prescribe a cholinesterase inhibitor. You may have seen it advertised on television. Its trade name is Aricept. Hopefully, it will help improve Maggie's memory, but don't expect miracles. Its effects aren't dramatic. I also have some literature to send home with you. I want you both to know that I will be available to answer any of your questions, and I'm sure you will have a few. I will be turning your day to day care back to Dr. Hardy, but I don't want you to think that I am abandoning you. If you need anything, don't hesitate to call."

It was a deathly quiet ride home. Maggie was too numb to cry for herself, but her heart ached for John. She longed to reassure him, to tell him not to worry, everything would be okay, but she couldn't. Nothing would ever be okay again. In less than an hour, Dr. Mason had changed their lives forever.

17

The "Big A". This diagnosis has made me realize what a precious, and easily ignored gift, this wonder of life truly is. We take it for granted, as if it is our due. I have been so self-serving that I've only realized it now since it has been threatened. I have taken so much for granted, my family, my home and even my job. I lived with the unshakable knowledge that I would wake up in the morning and the world would still be spinning on its axis, just for me. Well, I woke up just a few mornings ago and discovered that my job was gone and now it seems the rest of the world has abandoned me too.

I suppose it is normal to wonder "why me" after this kind of devastating diagnosis. Dr. Mason was very kind and he did his best to be supportive and encouraging, but there was no hiding the fact he had handed me a death sentence. There will not be a fairy tale ending at the end of this story.

I know it might sound strange, but if it was my destiny to suffer a terminal illness, why couldn't it have been cancer? Perhaps that is a ridiculous wish, but at least then, I would have a better understanding of my foe. There are so many treatments for cancer. Perhaps I could find a thread of hope. Alzheimer's leaves me none. Yet, if I believe in God and a divine destiny or power, and I do, then there must be a reason I was chosen for this incredible journey.

On the positive side, John and I are talking again, although the topic of conversation is far from pleasant. We are trying to decide how to tell the children. It's peculiar, it doesn't matter how old they are, when it comes to something like this, they are still children. John feels they should be told the truth immediately. I am tempted to put it off as long as possible. I am worried that the diagnosis will affect the way they treat me. I don't want them tiptoeing around me, or babying me as if I was already on my death bed, or worse yet, treating me like some kind of an addled brain idiot.

However, I suppose John is right (again). They are concerned about me and they know I have been seeing a doctor. They will expect some kind of answer to their questions. Lying isn't an option, is it? Besides, how long could we hide the truth from our son, the doctor.

I suppose we might as well bite the bullet and get this over with. We invited Katie, Craig and Michael over for dinner on Sunday and plan to tell them after the meal. There is no sense in spoiling everyone's appetites beforehand.

Maggie

~

Journal Entry

It was a grim dinner. John and I did our best to keep the conversation light, but an aura of grim anticipation enveloped everyone at the table. Despite the compliments about the exquisite cuisine, everyone's plate remained full. Apparently, eating was the last thing on everyone's mind. Katie helped me clear the table and there were enough leftovers to feed John and me for the next three days.

We gathered in the living room and John offered everyone a drink. No one declined. I chose the chair in the corner and did my best to disappear. The time had come to break the news. There was no turning back, and there was no way to begin. I looked at John with pleading eyes. I didn't want to lay the burden on his already taxed shoulders, but I wasn't capable of speaking the words.

John nodded in response. That man can read my mind. He took a deep drink of his Brandy Manhattan. A little liquid courage, I suppose. There is no easy way to break this kind of news to the people you love and my heart broke as I listened to John share the devastating diagnosis with our children.

I thought I had prepared myself for the worst, but I was terribly mistaken. Nothing could have prepared me for the pain and sorrow gleaming in their eyes. I watched helplessly as Katie collapsed into Craig's open arms. The sound of her mournful howls pierced my heart and will be engraved in my memory forever. Or will it? I longed to rush to her side, cradle my child in my arms and take it all back. I wanted to scream "April Fools", do anything to take back the moment, but it was too late. I was physically and emotionally paralyzed. I couldn't comfort her, so I left her in Craig's capable care.

Michael remained stoic. I suppose the way a good doctor should, but I saw the glint of moisture pooling in the corner of his eyes. I suspect he saved his real tears for later. He listened to everything John said and asked many questions, but he didn't seem surprised by the diagnosis.

John and I waited for the initial shock to wear off, as if that were possible. After several minutes, Katie wiped her tears and struggled to regain some semblance of control. Since the cat was out of the bag, we wanted to decide how much information to share with the grandchildren. It was an interesting, though painful, debate and I found myself joining the conversation with incredible ease. It was almost as if I was talking about someone else.

We eventually decided it would be best for Katie and Craig to explain the situation to Lonnie and Marcia. Michael volunteered to help them with the difficult task and they gratefully accepted. They were bound to have a lot of questions and he was certainly the most qualified to answer them. There are definite advantages in having a doctor in the family.

We all agreed that Jacob was too young to be told. He would be told on a "as needed basis". I felt as though I was in the middle of a covert operation. And I suppose, in a way, I was.

The discussion exhausted me, and as much as I love my family, and my heart broke for them, I was glad to see them go. Katie and Michael hugged me as if they were never going to see me again. I understood their feelings, but I cringed from the attention. I wanted to scream, "Hey, I am still here! Don't grieve for me yet!"

In reality, I knew we were on the threshold of a long and tearful final farewell.

Maggie

18

Journal Entry

I went to the public library today. I was shocked to find so many books about AD. I checked out several. I am determined to find out everything I can about this damn disease that is threatening to destroy my life. Dr. Mason encouraged me to keep my mind busy by writing and reading, so I'm just following doctor's orders. Right?

John found me in the den when he came home from work. He picked up a couple of the books, read the titles and sadly shook his head. He thinks I am torturing myself, but I believe that knowledge is power. How can I fight an enemy I don't understand?

I was shocked to learn that the disease was first described back in 1906 by Alois Alzheimer. I thought it was a new discovery. Despite years of research, the cause of the disease remains unknown. According to some of the statistics I read, there are over four million Americans afflicted with the disease. Studies show that approximately one out of ten people over the age of sixty-five and nearly half the population over the age of eighty-five are diagnosed with it. So, it seems I am just a youngster in my new club. Lucky me.

There seems to be a lot of conflicting information and statistics about AD, but most of the books I've read seem to agree that the average life expectancy for most patients is approximately eight years after the initial diagnosis, although, some people have been known to live up to twenty years. However, from what I've read about the

progression of this disease, I wouldn't call them the lucky ones. They may be alive, but they certainly aren't living. What should I pray for?
Maggie

~

"May I at least speak to Dr. Hardy alone?" Maggie hissed in a whisper that seemed to echo through the room.

"Will you try to control yourself? We don't need to make a scene in the waiting room. I told you there were some things I need to discuss with Dr. Hardy."

"John, you have to quit treating me like a child." Maggie pleaded. "Please try to understand. Dr. Hardy is my doctor. This is my appointment with him. Don't I have the right to some privacy?"

The nurse interrupted their quarrel by calling Maggie's name. Maggie moaned in exasperation as John shadowed her into the examining room. They waited in heated silence until Dr. Hardy came into the room.

A single glance at Maggie and John spoke volumes to Dr. Hardy. Their body language told the story. Maggie was angry, mad as hell to be accurate. Good, Dr. Hardy thought. She is a fighter. She will need to be. However, John was a different story. One might have guessed he was the patient by his appearance. He looked years older and the dark circles under his eyes were clear evidence of many sleepless nights and he looked as though he might be battling a hangover. It wasn't surprising, a diagnosis like Alzheimer's affected people in different ways.

Dr. Hardy smiled warmly and sat behind the small metal desk that sat in the corner of the room. It was a dramatic difference from Dr. Mason's office, but Maggie was more comfortable there. She knew Dr. Hardy and trusted him, and right now she needed all the support she could get.

"I have spoken to Dr. Mason and he has sent me copies of all of your test results. I see he has started you on Aricept. How is that going?" Dr. Hardy asked.

"Okay, I guess. It's hard to tell, but I think it may be helping. At least I haven't lost the house."

Dr. Hardy chuckled in response, while John glared at Maggie in shock and anger. "I don't think this is something to make jokes about. Dr. Hardy asked you a simple question, he expects an honest answer."

Maggie snapped. "No John. That's where you are wrong. This is definitely something to joke about. I'm sorry if I've inconvenienced you with my problem. I didn't mean to disrupt your perfect world. I'm sorry if you are worried and scared and I apologize for upsetting the kids. But damn it, this is happening to me! Why can't you understand that? I need to laugh, or I may start to cry and never stop. I need to sing and dance. I need to live ... NOW!"

Dr. Hardy fought the urge to applaud. He couldn't have said it better. "I heartily agree with your treatment plan Maggie. It is vital for you to remain active. Read, write, have lunch with friends, and continue to live as normally as possible. Don't be afraid to use whatever tools you need to make things easier for yourself. Write yourself notes, label cupboards and drawers, and use a calendar to remember the date. Don't be afraid to admit you have a memory problem. And most of all, don't be too embarrassed to ask for help. You must be willing to accept your family and friend's assistance. Don't push them away. As you probably realize, you are going to have good days and unfortunately some bad ones. It's all part of the disease. But it is imperative that you continue to live and enjoy life."

He turned his attention to John. "John, I know you are concerned and want to protect Maggie as much as possible. Believe me, I understand that and I sympathize with your feelings. But, Maggie is in the early stages of this disease and you both have a long row to hoe. You won't be any good to anyone if you burn yourself out now. There is no need to stand guard over her twenty-four hours a day, at least not yet, and we want Maggie to remain as independent as possible."

"I know that." John answered. "You know I only want what's best for Maggie."

"Yes, and I realize this is a very difficult time for you. AD is scary as hell and you're feelings are important. Do you have any questions or concerns you would like to discuss?"

"John leaned forward in his chair. "I do have a couple of questions."

"Okay. I'll do my best to answer them. What would you like to know?"

"Well, first of all, I was thinking of retiring from the bank. Do you think that might be a good idea?"

"I think that depends on your reasons. Are you ready to retire, both emotionally and financially, or are you simply reacting to Maggie's diagnosis? If that is your reason, I think it would be a huge mistake. Maggie can still manage on her own for a few hours each day.

If you enjoy your job and want to continue to work, I think you should. Of course, that will probably change in time, but we can cross that bridge when we come to it."

"Okay, that makes sense, but there is something else that concerns me. What about driving?"

Maggie gasped. She hadn't thought about that.

Dr. Hardy paused and rubbed his chin. "Now, that is a tough one. Legally speaking, there isn't any reason why she can't, as long as her driving skills are still adequate. However, safety is the issue. What do you think Maggie?"

Thank God someone was willing to listen to her opinion. She was beginning to feel like a fly on the wall. "Of course I can drive. I drove the car to the library yesterday." She answered defiantly. She glared at John with an icy stare. Would the betrayals ever end, or would she simply quit caring?

"Have you ever experienced any difficulties behind the wheel, such as understanding street signs or getting lost?" Dr. Hardy asked.

Maggie hesitated. "Well, I've never had any problems with street signs." She answered. Omission wasn't really telling a lie, she reassured herself.

Dr. Hardy studied her face as if he could read her mind. Maggie twitched nervously from his steady gaze. "Well, I think I'll refrain from making any decision on the driving issue until I have the opportunity to consult with Dr. Mason. I would really like to hear his opinion before I give you an answer. Until then, I think it would be best for Maggie to stay seated in the passenger seat."

Maggie bit her lip, while John sat up straighter and seemed excessively pleased with himself.

Dr. Hardy watched them with empathy. They were already exhausted and this was just the beginning. There would be tougher decisions to be made down the road, but they weren't prepared to face them yet. The wound was too fresh. He prayed the stress wouldn't drive them apart. He had seen it happen before. It was probably a good time to end the visit. They had covered enough painful ground for one day.

"Well, are there any other questions you would like to ask?"

"No, not at the moment." John answered.

Maggie shook her head. She had heard quite enough for one day, thank you very much. Somewhere, there was a cigarette with her name on it and she was going to find it.

"Okay, we will set you up with another appointment in about three months. Of course, if you need anything before that, don't hesitate to call."

19

I won this round. Dr. Hardy called and said I can continue to drive, with certain limitations, of course. I promised to limit my travels to short distances from home, and only to familiar places. (Believe me, I have learned my lesson there.)

John begrudgingly handed me back my car keys. It was a bittersweet victory. As I put them in my purse, I realized it was only a temporary reprieve. The day will come, way too soon, that I won't have a choice in the matter. But by then, I probably won't care.

Maggie

~

Journal Entry

I remember my first diary. It was a gift from my mother and father on my eighth birthday. There was a picture of three puppies on the front cover and it had a small gold lock on its side. Of course I told my mother that I loved it, but in truth, I was dreadfully disappointed. I was really hoping for a new bike. However, times were tough and the diary was the only thing my parents could afford. As it turned out, it was one of the best gifts I have ever received. My diary soon became my best friend. I wrote in it every day and I was always careful to hide it from prying eyes in my underwear drawer. It was the safest place I knew to hide an eight year old girl's secrets.

As the years went by, pictures of puppies were replaced by leather journals or spiral notebooks. The cover didn't matter, as long as there were welcoming blank pages to fill. My journal became my confidante. I could write anything without fear of being laughed at or judged.

Now that AD has entered my life, my journal has taken on a new importance to me. It has become my lifeline. No matter how vigorously I fight this enemy, in the end it will be the victor. There are still so many things I need to tell John and the rest of my family. Perhaps these pages will afford me that opportunity. I always thought there was plenty of time. Time to retire, time to travel, and time to watch my grandchildren grow. Now, the powers that be, tell me my time is limited. There isn't an endless supply of tomorrows. I must live in each and every moment.

I hope these pages will be a comfort to my family oneday. I want to be remembered as I am now, a wife, a mother and grandmother, but most of all as me. I pray they don't dwell on the empty shell this disease is destined to make me.

Maggie

~

Journal Entry

I try to go for a lot of walks these days. I say try, because John has cut down his hours at work and it isn't easy to escape the watchful eyes of the "Gestapo". I also find it to be a strange coincidence that Katie just happens to stop by while he is at work. I have tried to hold my tongue, but it is becoming more difficult. I resent their scheme to keep an eye on me. I may be sick, but I'm not stupid. I realize they are concerned about me, but I don't need a baby-sitter, at least not yet.

I wish I could make them understand that there are times I need to be alone. I don't think I'm depressed. I'm not sulking or feeling sorry for myself. I simply need time to think, to recall happier times and most of all, to escape their worried eyes.

If there is a blessing to be found in this disease, it would be my increased appreciation for the simple things in life I have always taken for granted. A walk in the park can be as restful as a vacation. I have found joy, sitting on a park bench and feeling the sun on my face.

I have learned to accept each day as a blessing and a gift from God. Yet, I feel Alzheimer's lurking like a thief in the night, patiently waiting for the opportunity to steal my mind and soul. Sometimes I am convinced that I can feel him, perched on my shoulder, snatching bits and pieces away from me. But I swear, I will not make it easy for him. I will fight him each step of the way.

Maggie

~

Journal Entry

The sky is falling! Everything is crashing down on me and I can't seem to stop this endless flood of tears. Suddenly, everything I see and hear is a resounding reminder of all I have to lose. My death doesn't frighten me, well perhaps a little, but it is the loss of control and the very loss of myself that terrifies me. What will I become? Who will I become? These are the questions that plague me. I have read some case studies that describe severe personality changes in Alzheimer's patients. Some patients become very violent. Will that happen to me?

I have tried to talk to John about it. I have so many questions. Will he put me in a nursing home? Has he even thought about what the future might bring? He refuses to discuss it. He says I worry too much and promises to take care of me. End of discussion.

I wish I could make him understand. I don't want to be placated like a contrary child. As difficult and distasteful as it is, I need to be realistic about my future, or should I say, my lack of one. I want to be involved with the decisions that will affect my life and death. Is that too much to ask?

I try to keep working my mind. I read everything I can get my hands on. I try to work crossword puzzles. I write in my journal and I've even found a chat room on the Internet with other AD patients and family members. On a good day, I can almost convince myself that I can beat this thing, but the bad days are brutal. I have a hard time finding words and I can't seem to do anything right.

I do my best not to upset John. He seems so angry. I don't blame him. I am angry too, but it isn't my fault that this is happening to us. Yet, I feel as if he blames me. I need him now, more than ever, but he pushes me away. We rarely talk and he doesn't include me in any of the household decisions any longer. And his cocktail hour seems to get earlier every day.

I ache to feel his strong arms around me. I hunger for the taste of his lips. I long for the comfort of his love, but he avoids my touch. Perhaps I'm expecting too much, or maybe I'm not expecting enough.

Please John, don't leave me now.

Maggie

20

Jerry Springer ended, and a timer buzzed in the kitchen. It was lunchtime. Perhaps it was a side effect of her medicine, or maybe it was AD itself raising its ugly head, but whatever the cause, Maggie seldom felt hungry and without reminders, she would simply forget to eat. She turned off the television and chuckled to herself. John would be shocked to find her watching "trash TV", as he called it, but she enjoyed the outrageous guests and their problems. It helped her forget her own troubles for an hour.

Maggie walked into the kitchen and gazed at the well labeled cupboard doors. Everything was organized, just for her. After a moment of consideration, she decided to have soup. She opened the cupboard marked canned goods and stared at its contents. There were so many choices. How could she possibly decide? Finally. She simply closed her eyes and randomly grabbed a can. She opened her eyes. Chicken noodle, not a bad choice.

She placed the can on the counter and read labels until she found the cupboard that held the soup bowls. Oh, she had been terribly insulted when Katie put up the labels, but she had to admit, if only to herself, that they were a Godsend. Next, she pulled open the utensil drawer and took out the can opener. She positioned it on the can and turned the handle. Nothing happened. She tried again with the same pitiful results. How did the damn thing work? She tried every position possible with no success. Tears of frustration and mounting anger pooled in her eyes. How could she be so stupid? A child could open a can.

Maggie never heard the back door open. Katie walked into the kitchen and found her mother, close to hysterics with a can opener gripped tightly in her hand. Sympathy and fear tore through Katie's heart. It was hard to believe she was watching the same woman she had depended on and admired her entire life. She hesitated only a moment before rushing to her mother's side.

Katie placed a loving hand on Maggie's shoulder. "Hi Mom. I was on my way to the grocery store and thought I'd stop by to see if there was anything you needed."

Maggie jumped. "Oh Katie, you startled me." She hastily wiped her tears and struggled to calm her racing heart. "I was thinking of making a can of soup for lunch, but I think a sandwich might be better. Would you like one?"

"No, I ate something before I came over..." Katie paused, suddenly understanding what must have caused Maggie's hysteria. "Mom, would you like me to open that can of soup for you?"

Maggie bit her bottom lip while a torrent of tears spilled down her cheeks. "Oh please. I tried and tried, but I couldn't make this damn thing work. I feel like a fool."

Katie gave Maggie a reassuring hug. "Don't worry about it. I'm happy to help. I promise, it's no big deal."

Maggie watched in embarrassed silence as Katie opened the can with ease. "Do you have a pan to cook it in?" Katie asked.

"No. Your father doesn't want me to use the stove when I am alone. I was going to microwave it in the soup bowl."

Katie nodded. That made sense, and she was comforted by the fact that her mother remembered the rule. She poured the soup into the bowl and popped it into the microwave. "Why don't you sit down and I'll finish this up for you. We'll visit while you have lunch."

Maggie meekly nodded and obediently took a seat at the table. Why did Katie have to see her this way? She was sure to tell John and he was bound to make a big deal out of this. Of course, everything was a big deal to him these days. She felt like a child who was caught with her hand in the cookie jar. "Just wait until your father gets home," resounded in her mind.

~

Journal Entry

It was just as I expected. Katie tattled on me the minute John came home from work. He was barely through the door when she hauled him into the den for a private chat. Do they think I am stupid? Of course I knew they were talking about me. I tried to listen at the door, but I could only hear the hum of their voices. I couldn't make out the actual words they were saying, but I really didn't have to.

Katie came out first. Guilt was written in capital letters on her face. She gave me a hasty hug and hightailed it out the door. I stepped into the den and found John. His face was flushed and he already had a drink in his hand. He totally ignored me as he walked past and went straight to my purse. He pocketed my car keys and I could tell by the look on his face that there was no sense in arguing about it. And the moral of the story is ... if you can't use a can opener, you can't drive a car.

Maggie

21

The world seems to be revolving backwards. I can't remember how to use a new fangled device like a can opener, yet old memories flood my mind as if they just happened yesterday. I've never really talked about my parents, although I regret that my children never had the opportunity to meet their grandparents.

My parents were the center of my world. I was their only child and there was never a doubt in my mind that I was loved. I was never the proverbial spoiled child. I didn't get everything I wanted, but then again, I never really wanted for anything. They weren't afraid of discipline, and they set some strict limits on me, but all in all, my childhood was a happy one.

The memories are so vivid I feel as though I could almost reach out and touch them. I recall sitting on our front steps, waiting as patiently as a five year old can for my daddy to come home. I didn't appreciate it then, but my father was probably the hardest working man I have ever met. He left for work long before I wiped the sleep from my eyes in the morning, and didn't return home until the sun dipped below the horizon. He worked at a local foundry. It must have been a miserable job, yet I never heard him complain.

My small heart jumped when I finally saw him coming up the walk. He was black, covered in soot, from head to toe. He must have been weary to the bone, but there was always a spring in his step when he saw me waiting for him. I can see him so clearly. He would drop his lunch bucket by his side and smile. His white teeth seemed to glow in contrast to his dirty face. He would pause for just a moment and then he would chase me around the yard, threatening to grab me in his filthy arms. I squealed in delight as I ran as fast as my small legs could carry me. To be honest, I wouldn't care if he had caught me. A little dirt didn't scare me. As far as I was concerned, he was everything a man should be. He was big and strong, but most importantly, he was kind and gentle, and he always had time for me.

I'll never forget the day my innocent world was shattered forever. It was a seemingly normal day, until I walked home from school. I was shocked to find my aunts, uncles, grandparents and most of the neighborhood gathered at my house. My aunt walked to me. Her grim expression caused my heart to skip a beat. She sat me down and told me that there had been an accident at the foundry. My dad had been killed in a fire. He saved three lives. He was a hero. Did she really think that would make me feel better? I didn't want a dead hero. I wanted my dad.

My mother never recovered from my father's death. Before he left us, I thought she was the most beautiful woman in the world. I would spend endless hours in front of the mirror, comparing my features to hers. People always said I looked just like her, but to me, I paled in comparison.

Everything changed after dad died. Mom just went through the motions of living. I was well taken care of, but the sparkle that made her so special was gone.

Perhaps I could have done more to help her, but I was selfish with my own grief. Eventually, the silence in the house made me realize how special their relationship had been. I missed the soothing sound of their voices, talking late into the night. I missed the musical sound of Mom's laughter when dad playfully swatted her bottom as she walked by. As time went by, it became painfully clear that I had lost my mother as well as my father. A very special part of her died with him.

~

Journal Entry

Knowing what I know now, I am almost certain my grandmother had Alzheimer's disease. Of course, back then we excused her behavior and called her a tad bit eccentric. Although the disease had been discovered, at least according to my research, I don't think many people were actually diagnosed with it. Most people were under the misguided belief that forgetfulness and confusion were simply an expected aspect of growing old.

I think about my grandmother now and I am so ashamed of myself. She was an embarrassment to me. I did my best to hide her from my friends. I was so young and foolish. I wish I could do it over again and tell her how much I loved her. Now, I worry that history will repeat itself and Lonnie, Marcia and Jacob will feel the same way about me.

My most vivid memory of my grandmother is a green dress and a pink cardigan sweater that she wore day after day. It was a fashion nightmare. It didn't matter what the weather was. It might have been a hundred degrees in the shade, but she would still have that ratty pink sweater on. Mom did her best to persuade grandma to wear something else. She bought her beautiful new dresses, but grandma flatly refused to change her clothes. She became so distraught each time the subject was brought up, Mom finally decided it simply wasn't worth the hassle.

Oh, how I wish I could do things differently. I can still picture how tired my mother looked. I could have done more to help her, but I suppose I was the typical teenager. I never considered how sad and lonely her life had become. Oh, the ignorance of youth. Forgive me for being so selfish.

As I think of it now, I realize it must have been a terribly depressing life for my mother, but she never complained. She was trapped in that grim and grief filled house day after day, with only grandma for company. Grandma chattered incessantly about the past. It used to drive me crazy. I can't imagine how mom survived it.

How will my family survive it?

Maggie

22

I despise this damn disease! I hate everything about it. I still try to read everything I can about it, but I'm beginning to believe John is probably right (again). Knowledge isn't power. Knowledge is depressing.

I'm doing my best to come to terms with the fact that the future doesn't hold much hope for me. When I was first diagnosed, I believed in miracles. Perhaps a cure would be discovered, or the doctors made a terrible mistake. This nightmare would end and my life would return to normal. Now, I realize I was being foolish. There will be no miracle cure in my lifetime, but I pray it happens soon for all victims who are bound to follow in my footsteps.

I'm not the only victim of this disease. My entire family is suffering because of AD. I am especially worried about John. Perhaps I've expected too much from him. He has always been so strong and in control, and I have always been able to count on his support, but not now. Unfortunately, he seems to be finding his strength from a bottle. I can understand the temptation to drown the pain and pretend Alzheimer's doesn't exist. But sadly, by ignoring the "Big A", he is also ignoring me.

Maggie

~

Journal Entry

Michael, Katie and Craig came over last night. It was the first time we talked openly and honestly with each other about the "Big A". It wasn't an easy conversation. There were a lot of tears, but there was some laughter as well. I think humor is a good survival tool. I must admit, it was a bit disconcerting to be the object of such honesty, and at times it felt as though we must be talking about someone else. I listened quietly as they all took turns describing behavior and mood changes that I can't even recall. I try so hard to concentrate and stay in control of my actions, but apparently, I'm not doing as well as I thought I was.

After a couple of cocktails, John finally broke down and shared some of his fears. He told us how difficult it was for him to watch me struggle. Yet, he forces himself to sit and watch. Sometimes, he has to literally sit on his hands to refrain from helping me. I can sympathize with his feelings, but I truly appreciate his restraint. It is vital that I stay as independent for as long as possible. As much as I despise the struggle, each success is so sweet.

He has been gallant in his efforts to protect me from his worries, but it is too much for him to face alone. I am still his wife and I pray I will be for a long time to come. Of course, my well being is his first concern, but finances are certainly a huge worry. We have both worked hard to save a nest egg for the future. Unfortunately, because of my situation, our retirement plans have changed dramatically. Even with insurance, our out of pocket medical expenses are bound to increase as the disease progresses. I read that the average cost for treatment per Alzheimer patient is somewhere around $174,000.00. According to that article, it is the third most expensive disease to treat. There goes the nest egg. I am so sorry John!

I believe in my heart that my family will survive, although I'm not entirely sure how. Logically, I know this isn't my fault. Yet, I feel so guilty for putting them through this kind of anguish. For now, I cling to my faith. Faith in the strength of my family and friends, but mostly my faith in God. I've never considered myself a religious person. And Alzheimer's has certainly challenged my limited faith, but I've found comfort in God's promise of a life after death. Someday I will be reunited with my family and I will be whole again. I denied him when I was first diagnosed, and I must admit, I still don't understand his motives. I have always tried to be a good person and I question why he has chosen to burden me and my family with this. But I tell myself, there must be a reason. There must be a reason.

Maggie

~

Journal Entry

John and I attended our first meeting of the local Alzheimer's Support Group. It was the first time since my initial diagnosis that I didn't feel so alone. They say almost everyone will be touched by Alzheimer's in their lifetime, either by having it themselves, or knowing someone diagnosed with it. Still, it was shocking to see so many people from our small community there.

We were both nervous, but we were made to feel welcome the moment we stepped into the room. It was an interesting mix of people.

Most of the people were family members, but there were a few AD patients there as well. It was a relief and a comfort to finally be able to share our thoughts and fears with people who truly understood us.

The majority of the members were there without their afflicted loved one. Many were still struggling with the many challenges of home care, while others were dealing with the trials and tribulations of nursing home placement. Fear and fatigue gleamed in their eyes and body posture. It made me wonder if John would someday wear that same haunted look. It saddens me to realize that I will be the cause of his suffering.

After a short program, we were invited to stay for a social hour. Coffee and cookies were served and it gave us the opportunity to visit more intimately with each other. We met another couple and we seemed to click immediately. Their names are Frank and Nancy. Nancy was diagnosed about the same time I was.

Life can be funny, and I don't mean to sound like a snob, but under normal circumstances, it is unlikely we would have ever met Frank and Nancy. Frank is a car mechanic and Nancy used to work at a local factory. Please don't misunderstand me. I don't believe they are beneath our social status. We have just spent our adult lives traveling in different social circles. Alzheimer's dissolves all the divisions of economic, gender or racial class. There are good people, and I suppose some bad, from all walks of life affected by this demon.

John and I agreed that the support group was a good experience. I am sure we will go again, although I'm not sure I want to become a regular member. I've never been much of a joiner. The only club I've ever really belonged to was the Book of the Month Club.

John said he would like to invite Frank and Nancy to dinner. To be honest, although I enjoyed visiting with them, I am hesitant to get too close. It may be nice to have someone to talk to and confide in, but how long will it last? What happens if we become good friends and Nancy suddenly declines? How would we deal with that horrifying glimpse into our own future?

The thought terrifies me.

Maggie

23

Has it truly been eight months since I was diagnosed with the "Big A"? Time sure flies when you're having fun. In many ways it seems like only yesterday that I first heard those terrifying words. Yet, in many other ways, it feels like a lifetime ago. And in many ways, I guess it was.

I sometimes wonder how much I have changed. It's hard for me to judge and of course, my family would never give me an honest answer. They are still in protective mode. I know I have declined. Reading is difficult for me now. I can make out the words, but it is a struggle to understand them. Thankfully, I'm still able to write with little difficulty. Isn't that odd?

John does most of the cooking and cleaning now, although he does let me help with the "safe" tasks. I am a master stirrer and duster. He makes an obvious point of keeping me away from sharp objects and heavy equipment, like vacuum cleaners (or can openers). I don't blame him. I have a hard time following the directions on a box of macaroni and cheese.

One day is pretty much like the rest and I find myself not knowing or caring what day it is. John put a huge calendar on the refrigerator and X's off the days, but it really doesn't matter. My life is one long weekend now.

I think I am holding my own physically, except I am so tired all of the time. I used to have so much energy. Now, it is a chore to get out of a chair. Dr. Hardy assures me this is normal. I sure wish someone would define normal for me. Believe me, nothing has been normal for eight months.

John officially retired last week. The bank threw a retirement party for him, but I'm afraid it wasn't much of a celebration. I didn't want to go, but he insisted. My presence just made everyone uncomfortable. What do you say to someone with Alzheimer's? Get well soon? I don't think so.

Retirement hasn't been a difficult adjustment for John. He hasn't spent much time at work these past two months any way. It's hard to believe there was a time we looked forward to our retirement. I used to dream about the day when we could spend more time with each other. But to be honest, the way things are now, John just gets on my nerves. God bless him. I know he doesn't mean to. He is just trying to be helpful, but he is constantly hovering over me. I snap at him more than I should and I know I hurt his feelings. I need to be more careful about that.

Maggie

~

Dr. Hardy listened to John's plan with an open mind, but he couldn't help but be concerned. "John, I understand your motives and I realize you want this to be a treat for Maggie, but have you really thought it through. Traveling with someone afflicted by Alzheimer's disease could be quite an adventure.

"I realize that." John agreed. "But you said yourself she is doing well, and she has always enjoyed our trips up north. The kids are able to join us, so I'll have plenty of help. I want to do something special for her, before it is too..." He paused and dropped his head. "Perhaps I'm just being selfish. I know this will be just one more forgotten memory for Maggie, but I'll remember and the kids and grandchildren will remember this time together. It's important to me Dr. Hardy, but if you think it is too much of a risk, I'll cancel my plans. I won't do anything to jeopardize Maggie's welfare. That's why I wanted to clear it with you first. Maggie doesn't know anything about this yet."

Dr. Hardy sighed. "I won't tell you not to go. I just want you to be aware of the risks. Make sure you take plenty of things to occupy Maggie with while you are traveling, magazines, a deck of cards, perhaps her favorite music. Plan plenty of rest stops. She is going to need some diversions from a long car ride or she'll probably get restless. However, try to avoid overly crowded places. They may agitate her. Also, you might want to warn the hotel that you are staying in that you are traveling with a memory impaired person. Most importantly, Maggie should always wear some sort of identification; a bracelet works well, with her name and yours as an emergency contact, and of course, the Alzheimer's diagnosis. This is a good safety net just in case she gets separated from you. Alzheimer's patients can have a tendency to wander off. Keep in mind, none of this will guarantee smooth sailing, but it may help."

"Thanks Doc. I'll be sure to follow your advice. We plan on leaving Friday morning and coming home on Tuesday. I'll call you to let you know how it went." John stood to go, suddenly anxious to tell Maggie the big surprise.

Dr. Hardy shook John's hand. "Take care John. And good luck."

~

Journal Entry

Well, John certainly blew me away this morning. First he presents me with a gift of jewelry. I had always heard that diamonds were a girls best friend, but in my case it was a lovely medic alert bracelet. Now, everyone I meet, can easily identify me as the loony lady who is losing her mind. But, that wasn't the only surprise. It seems we are going on a vacation. Oh, and it's not just the two of us, the entire family is coming. We are going up North.

I suppose I should be happy. I certainly don't want to burst John's bubble. I haven't seen him so excited about anything in a long while, but the whole idea terrifies me. I panic in the grocery store and I don't like to be too far from home. I suppose I should be grateful that we are traveling by car. They would have to hog tie me to get me into a plane.

This may be the most difficult phase of this disease. I'm so aware of my shortcomings, and despite my efforts to hang on, I feel myself slipping away. I think it might be easier not to be aware of my decline. Sometimes I wish I could just slip into a deep abyss where nothing mattered.

Maggie

~

Six o'clock Friday morning arrived with the promise of being a beautiful day. Katie and Craig pulled into the driveway with the kids still half asleep in the back seats of their van. Michael pulled in just a few minutes later.

After a short powwow and one last strategical examination of the map, they were good to go. Michael took the first shift behind the wheel of John and Maggie's car, while Katie and Craig followed in their mini-van. Each car had a cell phone for communicating with each other. Everyone, except Maggie, was excited to start the family adventure.

The small caravan rolled down the highway. Maggie's pulse began to race. Her anxiety mounted with each mile they traveled. The unfamiliar scenery frightened her and the car seemed to be closing in on her. She squirmed in her seat and did her best to quiet her discomfort.

John watched Maggie closely and noticed her pinched expression. "I think it may be time for us to stop for lunch." He suggested.

Michael glanced at Maggie and nodded in agreement. "Okay. Call Katie and let her know. I think there might be a truck stop a few miles up the road. We can stop there."

"A truck stop? Good. You know what they say..."

"...if truckers stop there, the food must be good." Maggie completed the sentence without opening her eyes.

John and Michael chuckled. "I guess I've said that a time or two before, huh?" John asked and gently massaged Maggie's shoulder.

Maggie relaxed a bit from the warmth of his touch and smiled. "At least a thousand times and I'm still not convinced it's true."

They pulled into the parking lot and climbed out of their respective vehicles. Maggie was just grateful to feel solid ground under her feet. She stretched and smiled as she watched Jacob's fascination with all of the eighteen-wheelers in the lot.

They were seated at a table located in the very center of the room. Lonnie and Marcia were continuing their argument over radio stations, while Jacob chattered nonstop about becoming a truck driver when he grew up. The men debated about what the shortest route to their destination would be. The discord was deafening to Maggie's ears. She couldn't focus on a single word that was being said. It was just a medley of unpleasant noise buzzing in her head. She bit her lip to squelch the impulse to scream and tell them all to shut-up.

She did her best to ignore their ramblings and picked up the menu with trembling hands. Glossy pictures and descriptive words promised an unforgettable dining experience. Her mind began to spin. How was one to choose? Did she want breakfast or lunch? They served breakfast twenty-four hours a day. Should she order from the Senior section or the regular menu? She fought to gain John's attention, confusion and embarrassment reflecting in her eyes.

Finally, John noticed her apprehension and immediately understood the problem. He patted her hand and leaned toward her. "Don't worry Honey, I will order for you." He whispered in her ear and pointed to a picture of a club sandwich that was one of Maggie's favorites.

Maggie nodded and slumped into her chair with relief. At least that was one hurdle overcome. It seemed an eternity, but their food finally came. However, eating didn't quiet this band of travelers. Lonnie and Marcia continued to argue over salt and ketchup. Katie was saying she was anxious to go to the craft shows. She wanted to find a new quilt for their bed. And the conversations from the diners surrounding their table buzzed in Maggie's head. She tried to focus on her lunch, but each bite of her sandwich assaulted her stomach, causing it to lurch in self-defense. She pushed her plate away in frustration and disgust, searching her surroundings for an escape route.

John watched Maggie with concerned attention. Doubt about the wisdom of their little adventure began to creep into his mind. Perhaps this hadn't been such a grand idea. Maggie was obviously distressed by the sights and the sounds of the truck stop. How could she endure the rest of the trip? He reached for the bottle of pills he carried in his pocket and offered Maggie a small white tablet, hoping it would be enough to calm her frazzled nerves. He briefly considered calling a halt to this selfish journey. How could he possibly enjoy himself if it was at Maggie's expense?

They returned to their vehicles and John's worries were quickly alleviated when Maggie closed her eyes and settled into a calm slumber. The miles slipped away and it wasn't long before they pulled into the driveway of a large country inn that was their destination.

24

The exterior of the Inn was breathtaking. It was a massive structure, painted a sunny yellow and trimmed with white shutters. Massive white columns supported the roof of a porch that completely surrounded the structure. The main building boasted ten guest suites, two restaurants and a lounge. It was an impressive building, that seemed to stand alone, frozen in time and space. Lush green forest surrounded acres of perfectly manicured lawns and gardens. Twelve cottages bordered the property's private golf course and swimming pool. One of them would be their home for the next few days.

John checked on Maggie and found her still sound asleep. "Michael, why don't you go check in and get the keys to our cottage. I'll stay here with your mother."

"Good idea. I'll be right back." He climbed out of the car and gave his body a well deserved stretch as he stopped to brief Katie and Craig on the plan.

After the papers were signed and the keys collected, the band of happy travelers parked in front of the cottage that would be their new home for the next three days. They unloaded the vehicles and decided on sleeping arrangements while Maggie slept, blissfully unaware in the car.

John gently rubbed Maggie's shoulder. "Wake up Honey, we're here."

Maggie stirred and instinctively brushed John's hand from her shoulder, as if she were shooing an irritating insect. Her eyes fluttered open. Startled, she quickly straightened and gazed at her new surroundings in surprise and wonder. "Where are we?" She asked, the remnants of sleep making her voice deep and husky.

John tenderly smoothed her cheek. "We are at the Inn. You fell asleep after lunch and napped the rest of the way here. We've already taken in the luggage. Come on in and see the cottage. I think you are going to love it." He took her by the hand and helped her out of the car.

Maggie's eyes widened in appreciation. The exterior of the cottage was lovely. A small porch with wicker furniture adorned the entrance. They walked through the front door and Maggie was embraced by the charm and simple beauty of the living area. An oval braided rug partially covered a well polished wood floor. The furniture was covered in brightly covered gingham and floral prints. Lace curtains allowed sunshine to gently warm the room. It was an enchanting area, but Maggie couldn't help but wonder if she might have appreciated it more a year ago.

John guided her to their bedroom, and once again she was enchanted by the simple charm of the room. A large feather bed with a whitewashed picket fence headboard dominated the room. Two over stuffed chairs sat in front of a large picture window that overlooked the well tended gardens. It was an inviting room and Maggie hoped her frazzled nerves would allow her the opportunity to enjoy it.

She glanced at John and smiled at his expression of youthful anticipation. He was as excited as a child on Christmas morning and she longed to share his sense of adventure, but a feeling of dread loomed heavy in her heart. This was a beautiful place, but she longed for the familiar walls and furnishings of her own home. An overwhelming wave of homesickness washed over her. She stifled the tears that threatened to fall, and kept her feelings to herself.

~

Maggie stepped out of the bathroom for the thirteenth time and paced the steps back to their bedroom. John watched her for the thirteenth time and felt a stab of guilt as he felt his irritation grow. Logically, he realized Maggie's behavior wasn't her fault, but her constant pacing was grinding on his nerves.

Michael sensed his father's discomfort and was quick to offer a diversion. "I'm feeling a little hungry. What do you think, should we hit the road and see what this town has to offer in the way of cuisine?"

Maggie heard the suggestion and stopped dead in her tracks. The mere thought of getting back in the car and going to another strange place panicked her. She was just beginning to feel comfortable in the cottage. She knew where the bathroom was and she didn't want to stray too far away from the safety of their bedroom.

"Doesn't the Inn have a restaurant?" Maggie anxiously asked.

"They have two." Katie quickly answered, noting the pinched expression on her mother's face. "We can stay here for dinner. I think the town will still be there tomorrow."

Katie's suggestion induced an immediate sigh of relief from Maggie. Unfortunately, it was met with vehement disappointment from Lonnie and Marcia who weren't nearly as enchanted with the country charm of the cottage or the Inn as the adults. They were anxious to spread their wings and explore the town.

Maggie swallowed hard. She didn't want to be a party-pooper. She forced a compliant smile and agreed to go into town. A tourist booklet offered a variety of recommendations and the group finally agreed on a seafood restaurant located on the opposite side of town.

After arriving at the restaurant, the first order of business was to have Katie show Maggie where the ladies room was located. Once that mission was accomplished, Maggie was able to relax and actually enjoy her dinner. The children were more subdued in the more formal atmosphere of the restaurant and Maggie fell into the easy conversation that flowed at their dinner table. The food was delicious and John even allowed her a glass of wine. For two hours she almost believed life was normal again.

After dinner, they made a quick tour of the town and mapped out a plan of attack for the next day. Much to her own surprise, Maggie found herself swept up in the excitement and was looking forward to the next days adventure.

They arrived back to the cottage in high spirits. Katie, Craig and Michael unanimously decided to go to the Inn's lounge for a nightcap and invited Maggie and John to join them. John glanced at Maggie. Fatigue was evident in her eyes. It had been a long day and he didn't want to over stimulate her, so he declined.

Lonnie, Marcia and Jacob retired to the room they shared to watch television, while John escorted Maggie to their bedroom. "You look tired." John said. "Why don't you slip into your nightgown and I'll tuck you into bed." Maggie gratefully obliged.

John tenderly covered her with the hand-stitched quilt and kissed her cheek. He stayed by her side until she drifted off to sleep. Watching her at rest had become one of his greatest pleasures. The worry lines that only recently etched themselves into her creamy complexion seemed to disappear and it was the only time she seemed at peace. He loved her deeply, and would gladly sacrifice his own life to save hers, but he knew he was powerless against this dogged assailant that was bent on stealing her from him. Time was both his friend and his foe. Every day was a gift, yet each day brought them closer to the end. He leaned forward and kissed her gently parted lips.

Confident that Maggie was fast asleep, John decided it would be safe to leave her for a short time. He told the kids to listen for their grandmother, and left to join the others for a well deserved drink.

25

Maggie woke with a start. Her vision blurred from sleep, she struggled to focus, but darkness enveloped her. She groped blindly towards John's side of the bed and found it empty. Where was he? This wasn't her bed. She struggled to remember, but her mind was blank. Her heart pounded against her chest as her terror mounted. Her bladder begged for release, but what should she do?

She tore off the quilt that loosely covered her and sat up. It felt as though she were dangling her legs over the edge of a cliff. Taking one deep breath for courage, Maggie inched her feet to the floor. Walking like a sleepwalker, with her arms extended in front of her, she stumbled through the black room. Her toe struck an unforgiving piece of furniture and she moaned from the pain. She inched forward until she found the safety of a wall and called John's name, but only silence answered her plea.

Her panic increased. Where was John, and why did he abandon her in this darkness? She couldn't catch her breath and the darkness started to spin. Dear God, her bladder was threatening to explode. The wall offered support and she clung to it has if her life depended on it. Carefully, she inched her way along its reassuring surface until her hip bumped something. She reached out and grasped a door knob with relief. Slowly, she opened the door to freedom and tenuously peeked through the crack, only to face more of the same dark unknown.

Standing in the door frame, Maggie listened. Did she hear voices? There was a patch of light gleaming beneath a distant door. The voices seemed to come from that room. Slowly, she aimed her body in that direction and tiptoed her way across the floor.

"John! John!" She cried out helplessly into the blackness. "Where are you? Please come help me!"

She was within inches of the beacon of light. Warily, she reached out for the doorknob, unsure of what may lie beyond, hoping against hope John would be there to rescue her from this black hell. Her fingertips grazed the doorknob just as the door burst open.

Maggie shrieked. Lonnie and Marcia stepped out of their bedroom and stood cautiously before their dazed grandmother. Suddenly, Maggie burst into tears. Lonnie warily approached her, while Marcia raced to the phone to call their mother.

"Grandma, are you okay?" Lonnie whispered. His voice quivered with fear. He was well aware of his grandma's problem. Lord knew, it seemed to be the only thing his mom talked about anymore, but he had never had to deal with one of her episodes alone before, and he was terrified. What if he did or said something wrong?

Maggie stopped short and stared at Lonnie. A blank expression veiled her face. She seemed lost, as if she didn't recognize him. She cocked her head to one side. "John?" She softly whispered.

"No, Grandma. I am Lonnie."

"Lonnie?" Maggie paused and tried to remember, but her mind was as dark as the night.

Lonnie moved warily forward, careful not to startle her. He heard Marcia hang up the phone and prayed the troops would arrive soon. How could this be happening? His own grandmother didn't even know who he was. He wasn't sure what to do, yet he felt as though he had to do something. She seemed so lost and afraid. He couldn't just ignore her. He took a deep breath for courage, reached out and gently laid his hand on her shoulder.

"It's okay Grandma." He soothed. "I am Lonnie. I'm your grandson. What can I do to help you?"

A glimmer of recognition flashed through Maggie's brain. "Oh Lonnie!" She wailed. "Please help me! I need to go! I need to go!"

"Where? Where do you need to go Grandma?" He asked in desperation. Damn, where was his mother? She should be here by now. He was quickly falling apart and Marcia was no help. She offered no assistance and stayed a comfortable distance away from the action, cowering and crying in the corner. Thank God Jacob was sleeping, this would be too much for his young eyes to see.

Maggie began a frantic dance, still desperate to find the bathroom, but she could no longer contain the fantastic pressure. She choked back a sob of humiliation as her bladder relaxed and released a warm stream of urine down her leg. She clutched herself to no avail. There was no stopping Niagara Falls. Sobbing uncontrollably, Maggie collapsed to the floor.

Lonnie and Marcia watched in horror. Thankfully, at that moment, the cottage door burst open and John rushed into the room. Glaring at his grandchildren, he unceremoniously pushed them out of the way. "What the hell happened here?" He growled, anger and accusation echoed thick in his voice. Both Lonnie and Marcia were too stunned to respond.

John fell to his knees, barely noticing the warm liquid that was soaking into his pant leg. Terrified and unsure of himself, he attempted to draw Maggie into his arms. Unfortunately, by this time, Maggie was hysterical and beyond simple consoling. His touch frightened her and she slapped his face and pushed him away.

"John! John!" Maggie howled, sounding like a wounded animal.

Tears spilled down John's cheeks. He wiped them away in anger. This was no time to show weakness. He had to be strong for Maggie's sake. Michael dropped to his knees next to him, his black bag by his side. Calmly, he filled a syringe and nodded to John. "This should calm her down, but I need you to hold her still."

Slowly and deliberately, John grasped Maggie's arm and held it still. Damn, she was strong. "Ssh, it's okay. I'm here. Don't worry sweetheart. Everything will be all right." He barely recognized the calm voice that flowed from his mouth, he was an emotional wreck inside. The sound of rushing blood thundered in his brain. His shirt was drenched with sweat and he was sitting in a pool of urine. The combination of odors gagged him, but he forced himself to remain calm. He had to, for Maggie's sake. "Maggie, I am John. I'm here now. Can you hear me?"

Maggie sucked in a ragged breath and turned her gaze toward him, recognition finally flickering in her eyes. She fell into John's arms. "Oh John." She sobbed. "I'm sorry. I'm so sorry."

Michael administered the shot and she never felt a thing.

~

Journal Entry

I'm exhausted and so very ashamed of myself. How can I ever face Lonnie and Marcia again? They must be horrified. Thank God Jacob slept through my disgrace. I don't remember very much of what happened, and perhaps in this instance, that is a blessing. It was bad enough to make John come home early. I'm glad the kids stayed on. Hopefully, they were able to salvage part of the vacation.

But truthfully, regardless of the reason, I'm glad to be home...
Maggie

~

Journal Entry

We had an impromptu visit with Dr. Hardy this morning. I didn't want to go. I am still too embarrassed to talk about my melt down, but John insisted on it.

Dr. Hardy checked me out from head to toe and pronounced me fit as a fiddle. Well, physically at least. He was a little concerned about my weight loss. I was thrilled. I've been trying to get rid of those fifteen stubborn pounds for years now, but I guess with AD, weight loss is something to be concerned about. But then again, what isn't? He told John to keep a close eye on my diet and intake. Believe me, that won't be a problem. John keeps a pretty close eye on every move I make these days.

He didn't seem surprised by the outcome of our vacation, but he did try to reassure us that this one incident didn't necessarily indicate that the devil, also known as AD, has advanced. He simply reinforced the importance of a stable routine and familiar surroundings. I couldn't agree with him more.

Everything Dr. Hardy said made me feel better. Unfortunately, I think it only managed to increase John's guilt. Poor John. This trip was supposed to be a special treat for the entire family. I know he would never admit it, but I think he thought it would be a sort of "last hurrah" before it's too late.

I feel so much better since we've come home. No more night terrors... And my pants have stayed dry.

Maggie

26

I am sitting behind my old electric typewriter for the first time in years. The computer has become too confusing to me and I think John has tired of coming to my rescue every other minute.

He has been so kind to me. He even put in a brand new ribbon for me. I didn't know they still made them.

I think John finally understands how important this journal is to me. It is both my escape and my legacy. Hopefully, these pages will help my love ones remember the "real" me, the person I was before AD came calling. And who knows, maybe my words will help someone else facing this grim future.

Maggie

~

Journal Entry

Dearest Katie,

I don't have to tell you that I love you. Thankfully, I'm confident that you know that and believe it to be true. It would be horrible to waste precious time, speaking the obvious. However, because of the limited future this disease promises me, I feel compelled to put these words to paper while I still can.

You are such a blessing to me. Sometimes, when my thoughts drift to the past, as they often do these days, I close my eyes and recall the wondrous feeling of holding you in my arms for the first time. Being a mother, you know what a heady experience that is yourself. You were a beautiful baby, perfect in every way. Of course, that is a completely unbiased statement. It was a miraculous moment for me. I was so proud of myself, one might have thought I invented childbirth. I was invincible. The future was bright in front of me. Thank God I didn't know.

It's too bad there isn't an owner's manual for babies. Or does Dr. Spock count? My mother was already gone when you were born, so I couldn't turn to her for advice. I'm sure I made more than my fair share of mistakes, but despite my blunders, you grew up to be a remarkable person. Now, before you get a big head from all of these compliments, let me say you weren't always an easy child. You were a handful from the moment you were born. Memories of your younger months are a blur to me. I don't think you slept longer than two hours at a time. Sleep became a luxury rather than a necessity. Thankfully, you weren't fussy. You just wanted to be where the action was.

Of course, it goes without saying that you were a genius. But, you were a late bloomer when it came to crawling. Not that you really needed to. Why crawl, when you could simply roll wherever you wanted to go? And you were fast. It was a waste of time to lay you on a blanket. If I turned my back on you for just a second, you would be gone. Sometimes, you would roll right into another room. I am laughing out loud as I write this.

You were always a good natured child. I was the envy of all of my friends. I could take you anywhere without worrying about silly tantrums. Don't get me wrong, you weren't a perfect angel, or anything close, but you were wise enough not to pick your battles in public. I wish I could say the same for your brother. Ha!

It's hard to believe that those days are over. Where did the time go? My baby girl is all grown up with children of her own. Now, more than ever, I long for the days when I could cradle you in my arms and comfort you from life's bumps and bruises. I suspect my disease may be hardest on you. In the long run, there are few relationships in life than can compete with that of mother and daughter. If I had the power, I would protect you from the brutal heartbreak of AD. Unfortunately, we both know that is impossible. Therefore, we must do our best to live each and every day to it's fullest. Allow me to take this time to thank you for each moment you have generously shared with me. I may forget, but your love and devotion will not be forgotten.

I don't want to be maudlin, that isn't what this letter is about. But, there are so many things still left unsaid. I need you to know how proud I am of you. You are an amazing person. And if my influence contributed in any way to that end, I am humbled. I love and envy your independence, your undying loyalty to family and friends, and your ability to find joy in everyday life. You are not only my daughter, you are my best friend.

It fills my heart with peace, knowing you have found an enduring love with Craig. At least I know you will always be taken care of (not that you can't take care of yourself). I'm fairly certain you won't agree with me, but I believe you and Craig should have had a dozen children. You were destined to be parents. In this very difficult time, when the world seems to be going to hell in a hand basket, you have managed to raise three very impressive young people. Sadly, I think it is rare to find young people who believe in the importance of love, kindness and truth. It breaks my heart to know I won't see them grow up and have children of their own. But, rest assured, I will be there. As long as you carry my memory in your heart, I will survive.

Be brave. You give me strength to carry on.

Love Forever and Beyond,

Mom

~

Journal Entry

John went to an Alzheimer's support group meeting last night. He begged me to join him, but I refused to go. He wasn't happy about it, especially since it was my idea to become involved in the program in the first place. Shockingly, after a brief argument, he relented and even let me stay home alone.

To be honest, I was afraid to go. I didn't want to face Frank. Nancy wasn't with him at the last meeting. She fell down a flight of stairs and broke her hip. The last we heard, she was still in the hospital. Frank said she was terribly confused. Apparently, she was fighting with the nurses and was totally uncooperative with her therapists. He wasn't sure when, or if, she would be released. Frank looks terrible. You can see this has taken a terrific toll on him. It must be hell, and I certainly sympathize, but it hits a little too close to home.

On the other hand, I am quite proud of myself. I managed to stay alone without any problems. Of course, Katie called me three times in two hours, but I can't blame her or John for checking on me, especially after what happened during our vacation. But, that was different. I feel safe at home.

I have to admit I really enjoyed having the house to myself. It seems that I never have a moment to myself any more. I tried to watch television, but I find it terribly frustrating. Everything moves too fast and I can't follow the plots.

So, I spent most of the time simply wandering through the house. There are so many wonderful memories hidden within these walls. I can still make out the marks on the door frame where we measured Katie and Michael's height. John thought I was silly, but when we remodeled, I couldn't bring myself to replace that trim. I made the right decision.

John came home and found me sitting in the dark. He probably thought that I had forgotten how to turn on the light. But the fact is, I just felt like sitting in the dark. Most likely, he was probably too relieved to find the house still standing to notice. I'm sure he was a nervous wreck during the meeting.

What a burden I've became to him. He has become an old man before my eyes.

I am so sorry.

Maggie

~

Journal Entry

Dear God, I am frightened. What will become of me? This damn disease is such a mystery, and it is the unknown that terrifies me the most. Yet, if someone offered me a glimpse into my future, I'm not sure I would accept the offer. Will I be blissfully unaware of my losses? Or, will I be trapped within my own mind, unable to communicate my thoughts or my needs? I don't want to merely exist. I pray God has the mercy to take me before that happens.

I know I am feeling sorry for myself and I try not to fall into that trap too often. It doesn't solve anything and it is a waste of precious time. Although it would be very easy to succumb to these feelings of despair and remain there. I certainly have the right to feel sorry for myself, but I want to enjoy each and every moment of every day.

So much to do... And so little time.

Maggie

27

Well, we've reached a milestone. I've just celebrated (poor choice of words) my first anniversary with Alzheimer's. To commemorate this solemn event, I had a checkup with Dr. Mason and Dr. Hardy. They both seem to think I am doing well. I would tend to agree with them, at least, on my good days.

I do fairly well as long as I stay close to home. Unfortunately, my self-imposed seclusion is one more burden for John. Now he is responsible for all of the shopping and other errands I used to take care of. Under different circumstances, I might take some greedy pleasure in that, but now it just increases my guilt.

I rarely go out in public. Even a trip to the doctor's office throws me off for a few days. The last time I went shopping with John, a lady approached us to say hello. I could tell by her greeting that she knew me. For the life of me, I couldn't remember who she was. Her discomfort around me was obvious, and after a brief exchange of pleasantries, she left. John told me it was Sheila, my old boss. How could I forget Sheila? I think I am still mad at her.

John asked if I wanted to plant flowers again this year. My first instinct was to say no. Last year, the flowers were a means to escape my fears. Now, I know there is no escape. However, the more I consider it, the more I realize it might be a fun thing to do together.

~

Journal Entry

I am exhausted, but tired has never felt so great! Katie and Jacob came over yesterday to help John and me plant flowers. Jacob stayed with me while John and Katie went flower shopping. Pretty neat, they left a six year old to baby-sit his grandmother. I don't care. I'll take him however I can get him. He is a joy to be around. Lonnie and Marcia tend to avoid me, and I guess I can't blame them. I doubt our relationship will ever be comfortable again. That saddens me. Echoes of my grandmother haunt me. On the other hand, Jacob still acts completely natural around me.

As far as I know, Jacob is still blissfully unaware of my illness. Lucky guy. If he notices anything different about me, he hasn't mentioned it. I think he just thinks I'm funny. We just make a game of my forgetfulness. Honestly, I think he is the best medicine for AD that was ever invented.

Okay, back to the flowers. John and Katie came home with a trunk full of beautiful flowers. There were so many, I couldn't imagine where to begin. Thank goodness Katie was there to help, because to be honest, I didn't do too much. Katie and John did most of the planting.

I teamed up with Jacob and we managed to put one planter together before we ended up in a huge water fight. It was great. I felt young again, and just like a child, I was scared to death that we were going to be in big trouble. Surprisingly, no one made an effort to stop us. John and Katie sat on the patio and watched, while Jacob and I chased each other around the yard, pouring water on each other.

Katie must have made a phone call, because Craig miraculously appeared with dry clothes for Jacob. While he changed, John helped me clean up. Sometimes I need help getting dressed. Clothes can be so confusing.

Craig grilled steaks for all of us. We ate on the patio and admired our handiwork. It was the perfect ending to the perfect day.

I hate to be greedy, but God, I would sure like a few more..
Maggie

~

Journal Entry
Dearest Michael,

I spend a lot of time looking at old picture albums these days. It is so easy to get lost in the past. I suppose it is less painful than looking to my future, or lack of one.

Looking at your baby pictures, brings back the wonderful memories of your birth. When the doctor announced you were a boy, your father and I collapsed into tears. We were thrilled. We had the perfect family. You were the spitting image of your sister. No offense to your masculinity intended. Ha! Now, as I look at your and Katie's baby pictures, I wish I had taken the time to label them better. I can't always tell who is who.

You may have looked just like your sister, but the similarities ended there. In most ways, you were her complete opposite. While Katie preferred to hang out with adults, many times to my chagrin, you could entertain yourself for hours with a few toys and your wild imagination. You enjoyed playing with other children, but it always had to be on your terms. You were the leader, even when you were too young to lead. Let's just say you liked to win. Now, I'm not implying that you cheated, but there must be some explanation as to why I can't recall you ever losing a game of Candyland or Chutes and Ladders. No one could be that lucky all of the time, or perhaps we should make a quick trip to Vegas.

At any rate, you had a stubborn streak that was a mile wide and a temper to match. Looking at you now, it is hard to believe, but you were quite a handful back then. Thankfully, you calmed down as time went by.

You were about ten years old when you first declared your intentions of becoming a doctor. I think it was after one of your many visits to Dr. Hardy for stitches. If I remember it clearly, it may have been the time they called me from school (again) to tell me you had hurt yourself. It seems you had dozed off during class with your chin propped on your hand. Unfortunately, your elbow slipped off the desk and your forehead slammed onto the corner of the desk. Four stitches later, you decided you were going to be a doctor. Okay, I'll admit that might not be the exact occasion, but it is a great story. And it is true. As for your career announcement, I paid no more attention to that, than I did the week before when you were determined to become an astronaut. But, look at you now. "My son, the doctor."

I hope you're not feeling picked on by this, because that certainly isn't my intent. I won't deny there was a time I wasn't sure my sanity would survive your childhood, but I wouldn't change a moment of it. You were like a shooting star in a dark sky. You made life interesting, and fun.

I have always been proud of you, but I think my proudest moment was the day you graduated from medical school. I thought my heart would burst from pride. Not because it gave me bragging lrights, but because you proved so many people wrong. Of course, your high school career didn't offer much hope. I must admit, I even had my doubts. But, I have never had any doubts about you, as a person. I know you are a good and gentle man.

I'm sure you suspected something was wrong with me long before I did, or was willing to admit it. That explains the covert phone calls with your father. Plus, you didn't seem surprised when we announced the diagnosis.

You have been my anchor. Thank you for your strength and support. You have been honest with me when I ask you questions about this damn disease, even though sometimes I don't like your answers. And a special thank you for suppressing the information I don't want, or need to know.

This must be pure hell for you. After all, you know better than the rest of us what this damn disease will eventually do to me. You have probably witnessed it firsthand with some of your patients.

I'm sorry you have to share the experience with your mother.

Thank you for being my son.

Love Always,

Mom

~

Journal Entry

I feel myself slipping away a little more each day. Writing this journal has become a terrible struggle, but I refuse to give up. John is helping me more and more with this labor of love. He has been so patient and kind. While my memory fades, my love for him continues to grow by leaps and bounds.

I spend hours in front of this typewriter, trying to put my jumbled thoughts into words. Then, John spends more hours still, trying to decipher and retype my ramblings.

...Thank you John.

Maggie

~

Journal Entry

Dear John,

What a sad salutation. This is probably the cruelest "Dear John" letter ever written. I feel myself leaving you a little more each day. The only way I can describe it is to liken myself to a completed jigsaw puzzle that is being taken apart piece by piece. Although I'm trying desperately to hang on, you and I both know I am losing the battle.

This blank page is daunting. Words I want to say escape me. Yet, in the end, there is only one thing I need to say. I love you, and sadly, I've already begun to miss you.

Perhaps it is denial, or maybe just good old-fashioned embarrassment, but I do my best to disguise my ever-increasing shortcomings. I know you see through my ruse. Thank you for playing along.

I am grateful for so many things. We have shared a wonderful life together. Except for this ending, I wouldn't change a thing. Looking back now, even our first dingy apartment and the countless meals of beanie-weenie casserole seem like paradise. Do you remember the "free" couch I picked up from the curb when we were first married? It sure looked nice and it was the perfect shade of blue. Unfortunately, I was young and foolish and still hadn't learned that few good things in life are free. How long did it take us to rid our apartment of fleas?

I'm thinking as I write this that it would be fabulous to be struck by a thunderbolt of inspiration, so I could at least leave you with a profound reason as to why this is happening to us. But, as of yet, that hasn't happened. Sadly, I have come to the conclusion that there isn't a greater meaning for our suffering. God didn't choose me for any more eminent purpose. It was just an unlucky draw of the cards. I never was any good at poker.

The one thing I know for sure is that I flatly refuse to say good-bye to you. I can't believe I will ever forget you. It is simply impossible. How could I possibly forget a love greater than Romeo and Juliet? No matter how tragically this disease ravishes my mind and body, you will always be with me. This has to be true, or kill me now.

Believe this to be genuine, I will always love you.

Maggie

28

The room was dark and the blankets were warm and cozy. Maggie curled into a fetal pose and was sorely tempted to suck her thumb. After all, if she felt like a helpless child, she might as well act like one. The infernal ticking of the alarm clock was driving her insane. But, digital clocks didn't tick, did they? Perhaps, it was the telling sound of the time bomb in her brain. It was just a matter of time before it would surely explode.

Oh, where were the toothpicks to prop in her eyes? She was determined to stay awake, terrified that sleep would release the demons that had been haunting her slumber. Despite her efforts, weariness won the battle. Her eye lids dropped. In the end, she was too exhausted to combat her fears. Maggie relinquished herself to sleep's mercy.

Buzzing, like a nasty swarm of insects, hummed in her ears. She flailed her arms, trying to shoo her invisible nemesis, to no avail. The sound amplified, louder and louder it grew, until Maggie was convinced her eardrums would explode from the sheer intensity of the sound. But wait, it wasn't humming at all. If she concentrated, she could make out the sound of voices, human voices. They were chanting something. There was a definite rhythm to the sound, but the words escaped her.

Suddenly, she felt entrapped, as if she were being surrounded. Terrified of what she might see, she forced her eyes open, half expecting to find the hooded figures of the Ku Klux Klan bearing down on her. But, there were no white sheets, nor any burning crosses threatening her. Instead, there was a tribe of faceless phantoms circling her, appearing to be dancing on air. She rubbed the sleep from her eyes and tried to focus on their faces. Slowly, the thick fog lifted and the mystery faces began to materialize and take on a recognizable form. Maggie's eyes widened in shock. Her heart thundered in her chest.

Could it be true? Her lost family circled her, their arms outstretched, beckoning her to join them. Oh Grandma, I can finally tell you how sorry I am. I love you. I understand everything now. Believe me, I understand.

Is that you, Daddy? Oh please come closer. Can I touch you? If this vision is truly you, give me one of your famous bear hugs. Oh, how I have dreamed of the strength of your arms. Carry me away from this nightmare. I know you can save me. You are a hero. Please, be mine.

Mom? Oh, you are so beautiful. The sparkle is back in your eyes. You must be so happy to be with daddy again. Can we go home now? Please answer me.

Suddenly, a blinding light exploded before her eyes. Maggie squeezed her eyes tightly shut. Gradually, the bright light faded and the red glow that illuminated her eyelids began to fade to black. Slowly and deliberately, she opened her eyes. Her chest tightened as tears filled her eyes. There was only darkness. The red LED display of her alarm clock was the only light in the room. They were gone. Everyone was gone. Maggie was alone once more.

Yet, she wasn't frightened. Everything felt warm and safe. Yes, everything would be fine now. She was sure of it. Daddy will take care of me. He knows what to do. She smiled to herself and faded into the night.

PART TWO

JOHN

29

I have never felt so tired. Oh, the nights are endless. I toss and turn until sleep finally comes. Days drift by in a thick fog.
I don't know what day it is. I don't care.

~

<u>Journal Entry</u>

It is with a sense of deep sorrow, that I can't begin to express, that I begin this journal entry. My dear sweet wife is no longer capable of filling these pages. I know how important this journal has been to her. Therefore, with a heavy heart, I will pick up the proverbial pen and vow to continue this story to its undoubtedly tragic conclusion.

Because of this damn disease called Alzheimer's, I have been forced to witness the destruction of the most dynamic person I have ever had the privilege of knowing. The woman I have loved for over forty years is now reduced to someone I barely recognize.

This is, without a doubt, the most tragic challenge I have ever faced.

John

~

<u>*Journal Entry*</u>

I was surprised by a visit from Frank this morning. I'm ashamed to say I haven't talked to him in several weeks. It seems Nancy isn't doing well at all. From what I understand about AD, and that isn't much, it isn't uncommon for a physical trauma, such as a fracture, to trigger a quick decline. However, that doesn't make it any easier.

He has transferred Nancy to a local nursing home. I got the impression that it will be a permanent placement. It broke my heart to listen to his tale. He sobbed as he spoke, wondering how he will survive this horror. The hospital bill, even with insurance, ate up the small savings they had in the bank. And now, he is worried that he may lose his job because of all the time he has missed. Of course, he feels guilty whenever he leaves Nancy's side. Apparently, she becomes very agitated whenever he is gone and they have to sedate her for her own protection.

I was more shocked to hear that his attorney suggested he divorce Nancy to try to protect the few assets he has left. Of course, Frank refuses to consider it, but what a sad state of affairs.

I feel terrible about it. Yet, I couldn't help but feel lucky that I wasn't in his shoes. That may not be a very Christian attitude, and I apologize for that, but it made me realize how fortunate we really are. By the grace of God, or by the luck of the draw (as Maggie might say), we could be in that same situation. However, his tale of woe did drive home the fact that there is no way of knowing what tomorrow might bring. Every day with Maggie is a true gift from God.

Unfortunately, I had no words of wisdom to offer him. My words of encouragement seemed empty and useless, but I gave him a sympathetic shoulder to cry on.

I sobbed when he left.

John

~

<u>Journal Entry</u>

GOD, WHERE ARE YOU?

John

~

It was another restless night and John watched Maggie with a sympathetic eye. He longed to comfort her, to ease her fears and the nightmares that haunted her, but he was impotent against them. In many ways, he was as lost as she was. He pulled her closer. She snuggled against him and they laid together like two spoons in a drawer.

He inhaled the familiar fragrance of her lotion and shampoo, and his heart quickened. His embraced tightened and his arousal grew. Unable to stop himself, he gently cupped her breast. Maggie's breath drew deep and she sighed. She instinctively pressed her bottom into the heart of his ardor. John groaned in response.

Months of deliberate restraint were welled up inside of him. He ached to hold her as a man holds a woman and totally consume her just one more time. Yet, he was afraid of destroying the magical spell that embraced them. Tenderly, he buried his face in her hair and gently kissed the back of her neck. Maggie hummed.

Gaining courage, John slowly rolled Maggie onto her back. Their eyes met and her mouth curled into a smile that both melted his heart and garnered his resolve to continue. He kissed her lips and she responded with a passion that amazed and consumed him. With surprising ease, he removed her nightgown and lovingly held her naked body close to his.

Maggie's eager touch transported him to another realm of time. A time when Alzheimer's didn't exist. There was no fear, and no doubts. He was simply a man making love with his beautiful wife. Nothing else mattered except the wondrous sensations of their union.

When it was over, they laid spent in each others arms. Maggie purred her contentment and drifted off to a gentle sleep.

I love you John. Thank you for loving me.

John kissed her forehead and carefully pulled away from her. Tears pooled in his eyes as the inevitable guilt quietly consumed him. My God, what have I done?

~

Journal Entry

How can I ever forgive myself? Do I even deserve forgiveness? I feel weak and humiliated. I allowed my physical desire to consume me. What kind of man would take advantage of a woman as vulnerable as Maggie?

I've tried to reassure myself that she responded to my touch. It wasn't rape. I didn't take her against her will. I simply reached out for the comfort of my wife's arms. But that knowledge does nothing to lessen my guilt. How can I be sure she understood what happened between us? She doesn't seem to remember anything about it. I would rather die than to think I did anything to hurt her.

Yet, I want her. I need her. I miss her.

John

30

My Dearest Darling,

It is a struggle every day to control the rage that threatens to consume me. Alzheimer's has left me physically and emotionally exhausted. Yet, I know this journey is far from over. I must carry on.

I watch you and wonder what you are thinking of. Communication has become so restricted lately. Even simple conversation seems difficult for you now. Silence surrounds us with a deafening roar. I miss the musical sound of your voice. Never again, will we debate politics or discuss the daily news. We will never critique another movie we enjoyed together. You can't begin to imagine how much I miss these simple things.

Yet, if I was given the choice of having you as you are now, or losing you completely, I would without a doubt, keep you by my side. Perhaps I'm being incredibly selfish. Am I asking you to suffer? Perhaps it would be kinder to pray for a swift ending to your pain. But, I can't help myself. I can't imagine living in a world without you in it.

I will stand by your side forever.

Love Always,

John

~

John rolled over and instinctively reached for Maggie. His eyes shot open as he groped the empty bed. He bolted upright, terror quickly choking his mind. "Maggie! Maggie, where are you?"
No answer.

His feet hit the bedroom floor running. The bathroom was the obvious start to his search. It was empty. The frenzied quest continued. Sweat dripped from his forehead. His stomach lurched, mounting nausea threatened to violently erupt. The house was completely dark and as he flooded each room in light, his heart dropped lower. Maggie was nowhere to be found. Where the hell could she be? Why hadn't he heard her leave the bed? He shouted her name until his voice was raw, but to no avail.

John, paused for a moment in the kitchen, trying to catch his ragged breath. Guilt for sleeping so soundly, overwhelmed him. What should he do? Should he call Katie? Should he call the police? He could hear the conversation now. Yes officer, I've seemed to misplace my wife. Could you help me find her? A chill ran down his spine. Where was that breeze coming from? He turned and noticed the back door was slightly ajar. His panic rose. My God, Maggie was outside. He raced into the backyard, desperate to find her. "Maggie! Maggie!" He shouted in desperation.

Terror fueled his imagination. She could be anywhere, wandering the streets, hit by a car, mugged by a thief, or worse. He searched the yard, the damp grass turning his bare feet into walking ice cubes. Beaten down and exhausted, John was ready to admit defeat and call the police when he realized he hadn't checked the garage.

His heart quickened with hope as he flipped on the light switch. Lo and behold, there she was. Maggie was crouched in the corner, partially hidden by gardening supplies. She was shivering from the cold, and fear blazed in her eyes. John approached her slowly and reached out to wipe the tears from her frozen cheeks. She was the picture of a child traumatized by a nightmare. Yet, John's heart soared at the sight of her. He held his arms out to her and she collapsed into his welcome embrace. He pulled her close and cried with relief and worry. She seemed so small and frail, she felt like a fallen sparrow in his arms.

Carefully, he lifted her into his arms and carried her to bed. He stood guard until dawn.

~

Journal Entry

Michael is here. He is going to stay for a few days. I have to admit, I am grateful for the help, and I'm sure Katie will appreciate the reprieve as well. She is a great help, but she has a family to care for as well.

I changed the locks on all of the doors and windows in the house, and installed a high tech alarm system. I pray they are too complicated for Maggie to operate, but I still don't feel safe. The nightmare of "that" night still haunt me. When I think of what might have happened, I feel sick to my stomach. Sleep evades me, though my body is pleading for relief. Now that Michael is here, I may just take a long nap.

Michael was obviously shocked by his mother's appearance. My heart broke as I watched him try to maintain a professional distance. Let me say, he failed miserably. His doctor persona quickly dissolved. He was just a son, trying desperately to face the heartbreak of watching his mother slip away.

He stared at her for a long moment before he approached her. He seemed to search her face, desperate to find something familiar to cling to. Tears of loss welled in his eyes as he attempted to speak to her. Maggie was able to answer very simple questions, but giggled like a nervous school girl through most of their exchange.

My heart breaks a little more each day.

John

~

John woke up. The glare of the morning sun streaming through the bedroom window startled him. What time was it? His stomach lurched when he realized Maggie was gone. The momentary panic attack ceased, as soon as he recalled that Michael was home.

The tantalizing aroma of fried bacon and brewed coffee triggered a rumbling in his stomach. Just like Pavlov's dogs, he thought. Grabbing his robe, he followed his nose into the kitchen.

Michael smiled as he handed his father a mug of hot black coffee. "I thought I'd let you sleep in this morning. No offense, but you looked like shit when I got here."

"No offense taken. I felt as bad as I looked. I must have felt pretty safe with you here though, I haven't slept this well for weeks.

Thanks for making breakfast. It will be a treat to eat someone else's cooking for a change."

"No problem. That's why I'm here."

Maggie watched the father and son exchange without comment. John smiled and kissed her cheek. "Good morning sunshine. How are you this morning?"

Maggie giggled. "Potato."

"What?" John asked, not sure he heard correctly.

"Potato." Maggie firmly repeated.

"Do you want a potato Mom?" Michael asked, turning to John for guidance.

John shrugged his shoulders. "You're guess is as good as mine. This is Jacob's game. I swear they have a secret language."

"Well, I wish he were here now." Michael answered in frustration.

"Potato!" Maggie demanded, pounding the table with her fist.

This action prompted a frenzied guessing game that left John and Michael desperate and confused. Hash browns weren't the answer, nor was anything else they offered. Maggie became more agitated with each passing moment. She glared at them as if they were fools for not understanding her simple request. She slammed her drinking glass down on the table and let out a piercing scream that could have raised the dead.

The drinking glass was the clue John needed. It flipped on the proverbial light bulb. He grabbed the glass and held up the carton of orange juice that had been sitting on the table. "Maggie, do you want more orange juice?"

A wide smile spread across Maggie's face. She nodded. "Potato." She confirmed.

John turned to his shell-shocked son. "Welcome to my world."

31

John's eyes shot open. What was that noise? Things that go bump in the night had taken on an entirely new meaning since Alzheimer's. He reached for Maggie. Gone...again. How in the hell did she do it? Perhaps she was a cat burglar in a past life. He turned on the light and checked the alarm clock. Three-thirty, much too early for Michael to be up. Well, at least she's in the house. The new locks and alarm system were a great investment. Moving slow, and feeling every minute of his age, John climbed out of bed to begin his search. Odd, the closet door was open. Was it open last night? He couldn't remember. He peeked inside. No, she wasn't hiding in there.

John slipped on his robe. Of course, he still worried, but he was becoming more accustomed to Maggie's night wanderings. He padded down the hall and noticed the bathroom light was on. Cautiously, he peeked around the corner. He had learned the hard way to approach Maggie slowly. Any sudden sound or movement terrified her. John smiled. God bless her, she was sitting on the toilet, trying to dress herself. Her best dress was on backwards, but she had managed to find the sleeves. That was quite an accomplishment. John's presence had so far gone unnoticed. She was far too involved in the task at hand. She was bent over, struggling valiantly with a pair of pantyhose.

John started to hum softly. Hoping, it would be enough to give Maggie warning of his presence, without scaring her. He entered the room slowly. "Maggie." He whispered.

Maggie jumped with a start and lifted her head to look at him. John's eyes widened and he tried to stifle a laugh. Maggie hadn't worn any type of make-up for months, yet there she was, dressed in her finest and made-up to the hilt. She recognized John immediately, another major accomplishment, and beamed with pride. Apparently, there had been a slight mix up between her lipstick and her eye brow pencil. She smiled at John with two perfectly drawn, bright red, eye brows.

Slapping his hand to his mouth, John attempted, without success, to muffle the chuckles that escaped his restraint. Lord, he didn't want to laugh at her. She was so proud of herself and he certainly didn't want to diminish this achievement, but he couldn't help himself. She looked funny.

His laughter brought Michael running. One look at his mother brought him to his knees. Their laughter must have been contagious, because it wasn't long before Maggie joined them. It felt good to laugh again and it took several minutes for them to regain some control.

John gripped his side. "You look very nice, Maggie." He fought the urge to wash her face. She was so damn proud of herself and it really didn't matter, no one beside himself and Michael would see her. "What are you doing?"

"Church." She answered.

"Are you going to church?" Michael asked, still grinning from ear to ear.

"Yes." She nodded emphatically.

"Maggie, it's Monday. There aren't services today."

"Church." Maggie insisted, stomping her foot for emphasis.

John glanced nervously at Michael hoping for some sort of emotional support. This wasn't going to be easy. Once Maggie zeroed in on something, it wasn't easy to dissuade her. She was becoming more childlike every day. Now, she had developed the annoying habit of throwing temper tantrums when she didn't get her way. Sometimes he felt more like the father of a spoiled brat, rather than the husband of a senior citizen. Unfortunately, it was easier to deal with a child that an AD patient. At least you could try to reason with a child. It was a challenge that kept him exhausted.

"Honey, what day of the week do they have church services? Do you remember?"

Maggie frowned as she pondered the question. "Sunday." She answered with a smile of triumph on her face. She knew she was right.

John smiled. "Very good. That's right. Do you know what day it is today?"

"Sunday. Church."

"No, today is Monday. We can't go to church today."

Her eyes narrowed in anger and John braced himself for the explosion that was bound to happen. Maggie clenched her fists and stormed John, howling in fury. John grabbed her hands and held them firmly. Maggie bucked against the physical restraint, thrashing and screaming obscenities. It took all of John's strength to maintain control. Although Maggie appeared to be a frail, elderly lady, she was as tenacious as a wild cat. John pulled her tight to his chest and held on for dear life until Maggie was too exhausted to continue. She finally collapsed against him.

John noticed Michael for the first time since the fracas began. Thank goodness there was a wall available to hold him up, because he appeared to be as limp as a wet noodle. Nothing, even his medical knowledge and experience, could have ever prepared him for the scene he just witnessed. This couldn't be real. This wasn't the mother he knew and loved. Yet, he knew the truth. He had witnessed it himself. How could his father possibly deal with this day in and day out? It was beyond comprehension. His heart practically burst with newfound love and admiration for his father's strength.

John smiled and shrugged his shoulders. "This is nothing. It's just another day in the life of Maggie and John." He held Maggie's arm in a firm yet gentle grasp and lead her into the kitchen. A large calendar hung on the refrigerator door. It was a nightly ritual to have Maggie X off the day before they went to bed.

"What day is it, Maggie?"

She stared at the calendar, the struggle in the bathroom apparently already forgotten. Placing her finger on the fresh new square, she thought a moment and said, "Monday."

"That is correct." John felt like a kindergarten teacher, complete with milk and cookies and naptime. "We can't go to church today, but we can go on Sunday. Okay?"

"Sunday." She repeated. Carefully she pointed to each square until Sunday, mouthing the numbers as she counted the days. "Six more sleeps."

John chuckled. "Sleeps" were the new standard gauge of counting days. It was an old habit of Jacob's and Maggie had recently adopted it. "Yes, six more sleeps and we can go to church."

"Promise?" Maggie asked, looking all the more like a child.

"Yes, I promise. Now, I guess since we are all up, we might as well have some breakfast."

John and Michael teamed up for breakfast duty. As Michael whisked the eggs, he whispered, "You're not really going to take her are you?"

"Hell no. Can you imagine what a fiasco that would be? Don't worry, She will forget all about it in an hour or so."

Famous last words of a fool.

32

Journal Entry

Once again, Maggie has surprised me. I would have bet the family farm that she would have forgotten all about this church business. Well, I was wrong.

It might make more sense to me if we were church going people, but I can't recall the last time we attended a church service that wasn't a wedding or a funeral. But, whatever the reason, this seems to be very important to her.

I promised to take her, and I have never broken a promise to her before, but the very thought of taking her terrifies me. I have seen her freak out at the grocery store. I can't imagine how she will handle a church service. Please don't misunderstand me, I am not concerned about being embarrassed by her. I just don't want to put her in a situation she is unable to handle.

I don't know what to do. Maybe it would be a good idea to get a professional opinion on this dilemma.

John

~

Journal Entry

I talked to Dr. Hardy. He laughed and gave me the go ahead. So, I guess we are going to church.

John

~

Journal Entry

I wish I were a more gifted writer. I'm not sure I have the capability to accurately describe the wonder of this day.

Katie came to the house early to help Maggie dress. They were in the bathroom forever, but if the sound of their laughter was any indication, Maggie was thoroughly enjoying herself. They sounded like two school girls getting ready for the prom.

Finally, the bathroom door opened and Maggie stepped out. She was a vision of loveliness that literally took my breath away. My Maggie had come home to me. She was thinner, but breathtakingly beautiful. She looked like a fashion model. Her image could have been on the cover of a magazine. Tears of love and gratitude filled my eyes.

Maggie chattered nonstop during the drive to the church. I must admit, I didn't understand everything she said, but she was happy and that was all that really mattered.

Butterflies fluttering in my stomach would be a poor description of my nervous status. It was much more like a swarm of killer bees attacking my insides. Despite Maggie's good mood, a multitude of possible scenarios played through my mind, and none of them were very reassuring. There was no way to predict how Maggie might react once she was around a crowd of people. But, I was committed to see it through, so I crossed my fingers and said a little prayer. It was show time.

As it turned out, my fears were unfounded. My shirt buttons nearly burst with pride. Several members of the congregation recognized us and came to greet us. They were probably shocked to see us there. It was obvious to me, but probably not to them, that Maggie didn't recognize them. She exchanged greetings and pleasantries with the grace of a true lady.

We entered the church just as the service was starting. Our family practically filled the last pew. That was a planned exit strategy, just in case we had to make a hasty escape. The minister droned on, and I must admit the meaning of his words eluded me. However, I was captivated by the expression on Maggie's face. She was so attentive, sitting very prim and proper with her hands folded in her lap. She appeared to be enraptured by the service. An expression of total calm and peace radiated from her face.

The Minster announced a hymn and Maggie responded without hesitation. I watched in complete disbelief as she reached for a hymnal and rose to her feet. I have watched her struggle to remember even the most basic of things. Yet, there she stood, her head held high, singing the words to the hymn from memory.

~

Journal Entry

My Dearest Darling,

If I have ever had doubts, or questioned the existence of God, it ended today. I may never know what called you back to the church.

Were you seeking God, or was he seeking you? It doesn't really matter. Today, I witnessed a miracle.

Hearing you sing in the shower or while you putter around the house has always brought a smile to my face. I've always known that you have a nice singing voice. But today, you harmonized with angels.

I will carry that moment in my heart forever.

I love you my angel. My life.

John

... And he walks with me, and he talks with me. And he tells me I am his own. And the joy we share as we tarry there. None other has ever known...

33

Dear God, this disease and it's consequences are relentless. Frank came to the house today. I'm not sure why he came here. We are certainly friends, but I never considered us to be that close. Perhaps he just needed a sympathetic ear and a safe place to vent his feelings. I was happy to lend him both, but damn, this hits too close to home.

Nancy passed away last night. It happened after the nurses put her to bed. Apparently, she tried to get out of bed without any assistance. Her legs must have become tangled in the bed rails and she fell, head first to the floor. Her nurse discovered her during the next scheduled bed check, but it was too late. Nancy was gone.

It goes without saying that Frank is devastated, but the situation is even more heart wrenching because he blames himself. He is convinced that if he could have afforded a better care facility, this never would have happened. It seems the nursing home Nancy was in had been cited for several violations during their last state inspection. One of those violations was for improper use of restraints. I didn't realize bed rails were considered a restraint. I always thought they were used to protect the patient. Frank explained that statistics prove there is a higher risk of injury when bed rails are used, especially with patients suffering from dementia. Unfortunately, he learned this too late.

Nancy just became another statistic.

John

~

Journal Entry

Dear Maggie,

My heart is breaking, once more. Will it ever end? My heart breaks for Frank and yet, I am crying for myself. I simply can't imagine living in a world without you.

I solemnly promise to always care for you. I pray it never happens, but if there comes a day when it is impossible, let me repeat impossible, to care for you at home, you can rest assured that I will seek out the best care in the world for you. Cost is no object.

The price Frank is paying is much too high.

John

~

Journal Entry

I can honestly say, I finally understand the definition of the expression "weary to the bone". I am so tired, I ache. Yesterday was an incredibly long day. Katie stayed with Maggie while I attended Nancy's funeral.

I met Frank's son, Martin. He seems very supportive, and I'm sure he is a great comfort to his father. He told me Frank plans to pursue a law suit against the nursing home. I don't think money is his motivation, although I'm sure he could use it. I prefer to think he is merely seeking justice for an unjust situation.

I wish him the best, and I wonder if I will ever see him again. I hope it isn't for Maggie's funeral.

John

~

Twinkle twinkle little star
How I wonder what you are
Up above the world so bright
Like a diamond in the night
Twinkle twinkle little star
How I wonder what you are

<u>*Journal Entry*</u>

Once again, when I feel as though I'm drowning in a sea of despair and hopelessness, my dear Maggie offers me a gift. Last night after we finished supper, we settled in the living room to watch some television. I must have dozed off in my recliner, and when I finally opened my eyes, the house was dark and there was no sign of Maggie. My heart began its familiar thumping from instant panic. (Maggie is a great cardio-exercise) How long had I slept? What time was it? Were the doors locked? Where the hell was Maggie?

I heard singing, and followed the melody to its source. Maggie was sitting alone in the dark dining room, staring out the window and softly singing "Twinkle Twinkle Little Star". She seemed so calm and content. I actually envied her. When was the last time I had taken the time to enjoy something as simple and magical as the stars in the sky? I couldn't remember.

I wasted no time. Grabbing a blanket from the linen closet, I took Maggie by her hand. We walked out to the backyard and Maggie smiled as I spread the blanket on the ground. Her smile melted my heart. It was such a simple thing, but Alzheimer's offers few rewards.

The sky was breathtakingly clear and the stars sparkled their brilliance like a million diamonds in the sky. We lowered ourselves onto the blanket and Maggie slipped her hand into mine. That simple gesture took my breath away. Neither one of us spoke a word. I have never known such peace, and I doubt I ever will again.

Once again, my darling has taught me an important lesson. Every moment we are given on this world is a precious gift. It's funny; things that used to seem to be so important seem petty now. It's wonderful to have a good job, a nice house and a new car, but in the long run, they don't mean anything, if you don't have someone to love and share it with.

I will treasure that moment of star gazing for the rest of my life. I pray God gives us the opportunity to share many more of those tender moments.

Dear Lord, hear my prayer...

John

34

John put the phone down and smiled. Somehow, despite Alzheimer's, life managed to go on. Lonnie was on his way over to show off his new car. John heard the car before he saw it, a new muffler was definitely in order, he chuckled to himself as Lonnie pulled into the driveway. He took Maggie by her hand and they walked outside.

"Come with me, Honey. Lonnie has a surprise for us. He just bought his first car. Isn't that exciting?"

Maggie smiled and meekly followed along.

Lonnie stood by his new prize possession, eager to show off his new set of wheels. It was the classic first car, certainly not much to look at, but Craig had checked it out and proclaimed it mechanically sound. Well, except for the muffler. Of course, Lonnie was blind to the dings, dents and rust. He was so proud, you would have thought he owned a Porsche.

Perhaps Maggie actually understood what was happening, but it was more likely that Lonnie's excitement was contagious. It was impossible to tell, but whatever the reason, she was acting like a child on Christmas morning. Her feet literally left the ground as she squealed with delight and clapped her hands together. John laughed. He was pleased she was enjoying the moment. Smiles were gold these days.

Unfortunately, Lonnie didn't appear to be as pleased with his grandmother's exuberance. His face flushed a bright pink as he glanced over his shoulder to make sure he wasn't being watched.

"Take me for a ride!" Maggie exclaimed.

John's heart warmed at the sight. It had been weeks since Maggie had been so animated. She seemed genuinely pleased for Lonnie.

Lonnie lowered his gaze to the ground and nervously shuffled his feet. "Gee, I would really like to Grandma, but I am supposed to meet some friends of mine down at the lake. Maybe I could come by tomorrow or something."

Maggie's magical smile vanished. "Please. I want to go for a ride. I really like your car Lonnie. Please..." She pleaded.

"I said, I can't right now. I'm sorry. I have to go now." Lonnie turned and reached for the door handle.

"Lonnie", John snapped. "Just take her around the block. It won't take long and it will make her happy."

Tears of shame welled in Lonnie's eyes. "I'm sorry Grandpa, I can't do it. What if some of my buddies see me?"

John's eyes narrowed. Now he understood where this was going and he had no intention of allowing Lonnie get away with it. "So what? What difference does that make?" He demanded an answer. Anger bubbled inside of him, and he felt like a volcano that was ready to erupt.

Lonnie dropped his head. He didn't dare face his grandfather's fiery gaze. "Well, you know ... What if Grandma does something weird and the guys see me? They would never let me live it down."

"Maggie, go into the house." John ordered, immediately regretting the tone of his voice.

Maggie bit her lower lip, but didn't move. John touched her arm and softened his voice. "Maggie, go into the house. I'll be right in. Lonnie will take you for a ride later on. Okay?"

Maggie's shoulders slumped as she turned to walk to the house. John watched, his heart breaking as she followed his cruel order. When she was safely out of earshot, John turned his attention back to a very frightened Lonnie. "What the hell is the matter with you. Do you see what you have done? She is crushed. How dare you hurt your grandmother that way."

Lonnie shrugged his shoulders. Old people just didn't understand. "Come on Grandpa, give me a break. My friends don't know that Grandma is crazy."

Crazy? Did he hear that correctly? How dare he use that word to describe his own grandmother! Something snapped inside of John, and before he could stop himself, or even consider trying, his hand reached out and connected solidly with Lonnie's cheek.

Lonnie stumbled backwards. Tears glistened in his eyes as he instinctively rubbed his stinging cheek.

"Get the hell away from my house and don't show your face here again until you can show your grandmother the respect she deserves." John turned on his heel, rage boiling in his gut, he cursed to himself as he stormed into the house. Lonnie's jalopy pulled away as he closed the door.

Thankfully, Maggie seemed fine. Perhaps there was a small blessing to AD. At least she could forget the hurt. John wouldn't be so lucky. This event would burn in his heart and mind forever. He loved his grandson, but he doubted he could ever forgive this. He kissed

Maggie's forehead and went to his den for privacy. This was one phone call he would gladly postpone forever, but he couldn't. How the hell was he going to explain it to Katie?

~

Journal Entry

Dear Lonnie,

I'm sorry things have come to this, but I will never apologize for my actions. I find your attitude to be reprehensible.

I realize you are young, but you are old enough to understand that you shouldn't, no mustn't, be ashamed of your grandmother. She is suffering from a disease. This is totally out of her control. Do you think she enjoys what is happening to her? She didn't ask for this and she certainly doesn't deserve it. However, above everything else, she deserves your understanding and respect.

You may be too young to understand every devastating aspect of this disease, but if you are old enough to drive, you are mature enough to realize that your grandmother would never do anything to intentionally embarrass you. She loves you with all of her heart and soul.

I have always considered you to be a kind young man. Never, in my wildest imagination, could I ever picture you as a bully. I would be willing to bet you would never make fun of, or hurt a fellow student that was less fortunate than yourself. What makes you think the rules are different for your grandmother?

I realize she has changed, and in many ways she isn't the same person you once knew. That must be very frightening for you. I know it is for me. But, try to imagine how terrifying it must be for her. Please, take a moment and try to put yourself in her position. Imagine, if you can, that you wake up tomorrow and you don't remember how to dress yourself, you don't know if you completed your homework, and you aren't even sure how to get to school. How would that make you feel? Pretty scared, I would imagine.

Now, let's take this one step farther. You no longer recognize your friends or your own parents. People you have known and cared about for years are suddenly strangers. Do you think you might be a little frightened? Do you think you may behave a little differently? I'm pretty damned sure you would.

Your behavior today has hurt me to a depth I can't begin to describe. Apparently, you aren't the young man I have always been so proud of. The grandson I know, could never be so cruel. I realize these are very harsh words and you may be hurt by them. But to be honest, I don't give a damn about your feelings. Your grandmother is my sole concern.

Hopefully, you will come to your senses. There comes a time when you have to bury your childish notions and face the real world like a man. That time is now. I pray you'll be strong enough to spend some quality time with this remarkable lady who happens to be your grandmother. I shudder to think how devastating it may be, if you wait until it is too late. This problem will not go away. It will never get better, I promise you, it will only get worse.

We need to embrace each other now, more than ever. Every moment we have with Maggie is precious. She told me, when she was first diagnosed, that she wanted no regrets, not for herself, nor anyone else.

Please Lonnie, don't do it for me, or even your grandmother. Do it for yourself. Consider what you may be losing forever, if you don't.

Grandpa

~

Journal Entry

Lonnie returned. Apparently, Katie had a few choice words for him when he came home. Judging from his actions and new attitude, she must have succeeded in driving her message home. I was pleased to find him very contrite.

He invited Maggie for a ride and she was thrilled. They only went a few blocks, but it was enough to satisfy her curiosity. They were both laughing when they returned and it warmed my heart.

This is how it should be, the way it has to be. There is no time to waste with unrest within the family. We need to stick together.

God help me. I need all of their strength.

John

~

<u>*Journal Entry*</u>

I considered destroying my last two journal entries. It occurred to me that Lonnie may someday read these words and find them very cruel. However, after thinking about it, I realized it would be dishonest to delete them.

There is nothing pretty about Alzheimer's Disease. This journal would be a waste of time and effort if I tried to gloss over the ugly seeds this disease sows. Maggie is not the only victim. We all are. Every person who has ever known and loved her is suffering, and will continue to suffer, long after she is gone.

So, the entries remain, as will all the other painful words to follow.

John

35

It was a good day. And believe me, I thank God for each and every one of them. Katie, Craig, and the kids came over. Thankfully, Maggie was on her best behavior. That in itself makes it easier to enjoy company, especially Lonnie and Marcia. I realize they are kids, and perhaps I expect too much, but it still angers me to see how they avoid their grandmother. Watching the way they act, one would think that Maggie was contagious. I only pray that Maggie isn't aware of it. It would break her heart.

Craig and I were able to have a heart to heart about it. Both he and Katie have tried to talk to them about their attitudes, but they are understandably frightened. There is no denying AD is terrifying. I just want them to realize that their actions now, may haunt them for the rest of their lives. I want them to cherish everything their grandmother has to offer, before it is too late.

Thank God for Jacob, He is a godsend and my hero. If he notices anything different about his grandma (and he must), he doesn't show it. If anything, I think they are closer now than they have ever been. I mean no insult to Maggie, and it may seem like an odd thing to say, but they interact like playmates.

There has been a drastic decline in Maggie's physical and mental abilities. But, the good news is, it no longer seems to bother her. I don't think she is aware of how much she has already lost. While that may be a hidden blessing for her, it is heartbreaking for the rest of us.

Katie approached me after dinner. I am smiling as I think of it. She is getting quite proficient at giving her old man lectures. She worries about me almost as much as she worried about her mother. It seems she is worried about my social life, or lack of one. She wants me to get out more and spend some time away from the house (and Alzheimer's). She offered to stay with Maggie so I could catch up with old friends or see a movie. It is a generous offer, but she already comes over several times a week so I can do the grocery shopping and run errands. How can I expect her to do more?

Apparently, she expected me to refuse her offer, because she came armed with a truckload of alternatives. I have to give her credit. She certainly did her homework. She had a stack of brochures for various programs she thought I should consider. One was for an adult daycare program, Maggie could attend several times a week. It offered a variety of activities such as games and craft projects to entertain their guests. To be honest, it doesn't sound like something Maggie would enjoy. Although who knows, Maggie has given me a lot of surprises lately.

Another option she suggested was to hire someone to come to the house and stay with Maggie. She showed me a pamphlet that described the wide variety of services that are available. You can hire a companion, or if you desire more nursing services, you can request a home health aid. They come to your house and help with daily cares such as bathing. Some services even offer assistance with some light housekeeping. I don't want to sound selfish, but it does sound tempting.

I promised to take a look at the information and to keep an open mind, but I didn't promise anything. As I said before, I have serious doubts about the daycare. Maggie gets so anxious when she is away from home. Her doctor appointments are a nightmare. However, I might consider hiring someone to come to the house. It would have to be a very special person though. I couldn't leave my Maggie with just anyone. It's a shame Jacob wasn't older, he would be perfect for the job.

John

~

Journal Entry

Maggie has been chattering nonstop all day. While I certainly prefer that to her silent sullen days, I can't help but wonder what triggers these rendezvous with the past. In this case, I think Jacob's excitement over his upcoming sleep over was probably the instigator. AD can be quite amazing. Most of the time, Maggie has difficulty recalling something that happened fifteen minutes ago, yet there are things from the distant past she can describe with vivid detail.

She has been talking about one of Katie's pajama parties. I haven't thought about it in years. I'll have to ask Katie if she remembers it. Maggie certainly does.

Here's the story. Katie was in the second grade. One day she comes home with a note from her teacher. Apparently, she had invited two of her little friends over that Friday night. This was the first surprise. The note went on to say that it was school policy that if an invitation of this sort was made on school grounds, all of the girls in class should be invited. This made perfect sense; you wouldn't want any hurt feelings. However, Katie had neglected to mention any of these plans to either her mother or myself.

I remember coming home from school that evening. Maggie was fit to be tied. She met me at the door and literally threw that note in my face. I, being the ignorant husband, read the note and started to laugh (wrong thing to do). Of course, my stupidity only added fuel to the fire. To be honest, as long as it wasn't aimed at me, I always enjoyed seeing Maggie fired up. She was such a spitfire, and the blush of anger made her even more beautiful.

In reality, the situation really wasn't a laughing matter and Maggie had good cause to be angry. Katie had managed to put us in a really tough spot. Of course, a seven year old has no concept of economics, but money was really tight back then. The prospect of hosting a pajama party for twelve hungry little girls wasn't in our budget that week (or any week for that matter). Being the pragmatic one, I thought the solution was simple, tell Katie she couldn't have the party. After all, she had no right to make those sort of plans without asking us first. End of story.

But Maggie would have none of that. Of course, she agreed that Katie was wrong, but she didn't want Katie to be humiliated in front of her friends. So, being Maggie, instead of punishing her wayward daughter, she did everything in her power to make sure Katie not only had a party ... She had a great party.

I didn't agree with her methods, and I'll admit a few voices were raised, but Maggie was quite amazing. She took the money that was meant to pay our utility bills that month to cover the expenses for Katie's little shindig. Of course, we had to skimp and save the entire next month to make up for it. Maggie convinced me that some things were more important than paying a bill on time, not any easy argument to win with a banker. No wonder she was president of her High School's debating team. Looking back, I have to say she was absolutely right.

These are the memories I long to cling to. Thank God I have Maggie to show me the way. We all need to treasure the special moments we have shared, and try not to dwell on the magnificent loss that looms before us. It will take a great deal of courage, but we must follow Maggie's example.

She is the bravest person I know.

John

36

"I'm missing a branch." Lonnie grumbled. What a waste of time. He had better things to do. His friends were all at the mall having a good time while he was stuck at his grandparents, putting up a fake Christmas tree. He was doing it, but that didn't mean he had to like it.

"No you're not, you dumb ass. You've put it together wrong. Look, you have some of the long branches on the top. Jeez, don't you know what a Christmas tree looks like?" Marcia teased.

"Yeah. They grow in the ground, they don't come from a cardboard box. Screw it. I don't need this shit." Lonnie threw down a branch and walked away.

"Hey, watch your language." Katie admonished as she playfully swatted his adolescent behind. "Grumbling won't get you out of this any quicker, so you may as well grin and bear it. Besides, Marcia is right. You did put the tree together wrong. Now, go fix it, or I will sic Grandpa on you."

John and Craig entered the living room, struggling with a mountain of boxes filled with Christmas decorations. John looked at the tree and laughed. "What the hell happened to the tree?"

"Lonnie." Marcia answered and giggled.

"Oh." John smiled, as if that explained everything. "I brought up everything that was marked Christmas. God only knows what is in all of these boxes. Maggie always took care of the decorating."

Katie broke into the boxes with delight. She brought out a few handmade ornaments and laughed. "I can't believe you saved these. Michael and I made these when we were in grade school."

John smiled wistfully and gently massaged Katie's shoulders. "You know your mother. These were her greatest treasures. They were far more precious to her than any store bought decorations."

Katie turned to her mother, who had been watching silently from her seat on the sofa. Nostalgic tears filled her eyes as she lifted the box and laid it tenderly on Maggie's lap. Maggie smiled as she poked through the carefully wrapped ornaments.

The room turned silent as the entire family watched in awe as Maggie tenderly unwrapped each priceless treasure. Tears rolled unhindered down her enraptured face as she revealed nearly forty years of collected memories.

Joy filled Maggie's heart as each loving memory flooded her mind. She longed to speak, but the words wouldn't come. The words were gone ... They were gone...

~

Journal Entry

My dearest Maggie,

I must confess. Once again, I am guilty of taking you for granted. As I look back on all of the Christmas celebrations we have shared together, I can only remember how special you made the holidays for everyone. I never took the time to consider how much work went into the preparations. Yet, you made it seem so easy and you never complained. As a matter of fact, you seemed to relish every moment of it. However, now that the job has landed on my lap, I feel terribly inept. How can I make this Christmas special for you?

I feel you slipping away from me a little more each day. I would never say the words out loud, but I fear this may be the last Christmas I will ever share with you. You are so quiet now. Is that your choice? I pray it is. I can't bear to consider the possibility that you are a prisoner of this silence.

Yet, I take comfort in your peaceful expression. At least you seem content. But I can't help but wonder if this is how you will finally leave me. Will you silently drift away? I am not ready for this. Please give me more time. Give me a clue as to how I can reach you. Even a brief smile gives me hope that you are still with me.

Most families will take Christmas for granted this season, confident that there will be many more to come. For many, it is just a hassle and a financial burden they have to survive once a year. Unfortunately, my family has learned the hard way that life offers no guarantees. Christmas has taken on a whole new meaning this year.

Maggie, I would love to share a thousand more Christmases with you, but that would be impossible even without the evil shadow of Alzheimer's. Because I love you more than life itself, this year I want to make a Christmas memory in honor of you.

Merry Christmas, my darling.

John

~

A layer of newly fallen snow made the world sparkle. It was a picture postcard type of Christmas morning. A new day and a new beginning... John followed an enticing aroma into the kitchen where Katie and Michael were busy preparing the Christmas feast. John happily accepted their offer to cook. Although he realized they probably had their own selfish agenda. John wasn't known as the world's greatest chef.

The sight welcomed him, and caused him to stop dead in his tracks. Katie was basting the turkey. Michael was stirring a pot on the stove. That was a heartwarming sight to be sure, but what stirred the lump in his throat was Maggie. She was sitting at the kitchen table with a mountain of potatoes in front of her, carefully peeling the one in her hand. She stopped briefly when she noticed John and grinned from ear to ear.

The meal was delicious and of course, the potatoes were the best ever peeled. Everyone ate until they nearly burst at the seams. Even Maggie cleaned her plate, which was reason enough to celebrate.

"Come on Lonnie, let's clean up and let the old folks rest awhile." Marcia coaxed as she started clearing the table.

"Okey dokey." Lonnie said as he jumped up and stacked some empty plates without an argument.

John arched an eyebrow in surprise. "Santa must have been very good to them. Or did Michael drug their turkey? I've never seen those two offer to do dishes before."

Katie shrugged her shoulders. "Every now and then they surprise me too. Maybe there is hope for them after all."

The dishes were washed and put away. The mountain of gifts were finally opened to everyone's satisfaction. Wrapping paper and brightly colored bows littered the living room floor. After all of the exhausting preparation and hoopla, once again Christmas was over in a few short hours. John was exhausted, but content. It had been a fine Christmas.

Suddenly, Jacob appeared from behind the tree, struggling with a box that was nearly as large as he was. The wrapping was mismatched and he must have used an entire roll of tape to secure it in place. He had a mischievous grin on his face as presented his precious gift to his grandmother. He gently place the huge box in Maggie's lap and sat down next to her.

Everyone watched with bated breath as Jacob urged Maggie to open her gift. She gently lifted the lid and peeked inside.

John watched and noticed that Maggie seemed bewildered by the gift. His curiosity finally got the better of him and he leaned over and peered into the box. He was shocked and appalled to find the box was empty. Anger spread like wildfire through his veins. What kind of cruel joke was Jacob playing on his grandmother? Thankfully Jacob began to speak before John had the opportunity to begin the verbal lashing that was perched on the tip of his tongue.

Jacob wrapped his chubby arms around Maggie and gave her a tremendous hug. "I didn't have much money to buy you a gift, but mom says it isn't how much a present costs that makes it special. I wanted to give you something to show you how much I love you. I tried and tried to think of something, but I couldn't. Nothing was good enough. Then, I remembered how you told me that my hugs and kisses were the best gift of all. So, I found the biggest box I could, and wrapped it with the prettiest paper I could find. Then, I prayed to God to fill the box with love and hugs and kisses from me. Now, whenever you feel sad or lonely, you can open the box and have a hug and kiss from me. It is a magic box. I love you Grandma."

There wasn't a dry eye in the house. Maggie might not have understood everything that Jacob said, but she obviously grasped the meaning behind his words. She reached for Jacob and held him tight in her arms. Tears of love rolled down their cheeks as they shared a very special embrace.

It was truly a Christmas to remember. And once again, it was thanks to a child...

37

I hired a home health care aide. She works through a private agency and her references are impeccable. Her name is Laura Jacobsen. I would guess her to be in her early forties, but what do I know? I was raised to never guess a lady's age. She has been working in health care for over fifteen years and has a lot of experience with Alzheimer's and dementia. I suppose I should find that reassuring, but I still have my doubts about this.

Of course, Katie and Michael think it is a great idea. I must admit, it is getting increasingly difficult to care for Maggie. Mornings are nothing short of a nightmare. She fights me the entire time I try to help her wash and dress. It's a struggle to get her to brush her teeth. This is so out of Maggie's character, she always took great pride in her appearance.

A helping hand might be welcome. It might sound strange after all of our years together, but I'm not entirely comfortable with assisting her with her intimate cares.

This seems to be a good idea. I know a lot of members of the support group have done it and they are thrilled. So, why do I feel so guilty?

John

~

"John, why don't you go do something. It's a beautiful day and there's no need for you to be cooped up while I'm here. Besides, it doesn't make sense to pay me if you won't allow me to do my job." Laura smiled reassuringly. She had been through this a hundred times. For the family member, the first time out the door was like leaving a child on the first day of school.

John thought of a thousand excuses to stay, but he knew Laura was right and finally relented. He gave Maggie a quick peck on the cheek and forced his feet to take him out of the door. Unfortunately, he hadn't had the foresight to make any plans for his new found leisure time. He was on his own with nothing to do and nowhere to go.

John chuckled as he drove. Life was funny. Part of the reason he hired Laura was because he was afraid he was becoming too dependent on Katie. Yet, here he was, pulling into her driveway.

Katie laughed when she opened the door. John grinned sheepishly. "Okay, I'll admit it. I feel like a fool. Here I am, a man about town with no place to go."

"Oh Dad, you know you are always welcome here. Come in and I'll put on a fresh pot of coffee."

John followed her to the cozy kitchen that reflected Katie's warm and inviting personality. He sighed as he took a chair at the table. "You have no idea how hard it was to leave Maggie with a complete stranger."

"Come on Dad, Laura isn't a complete stranger. You said yourself that she seemed very capable and she has excellent references. Besides, Mom seems to like her. It's about time you let her do her job."

"I know. You're right. Well, at least part of me believes that, but Maggie doesn't understand why Laura is there. She is a total stranger to her. I don't know if this was the right thing to do. I feel so damn guilty. What made me think I had the right to put my selfish desires above Maggie's needs? How can I justify leaving her feeling lost and abandoned just so I can have a cup of coffee in peace? It just doesn't feel right to me."

"Dad, I understand how you feel, but give yourself a break. You aren't doing anything wrong. You can't stay holed up in that house twenty-four hours a day. It isn't healthy. You have to take care of yourself or you won't be any good to anyone, especially Mom."

John listened with half an ear. It was the same pep talk he had heard a thousand times and it was hogwash. His place was by Maggie's side, not across town sipping coffee and eating cookies. Maggie was the only one that mattered. She was his wife and the mother of his children. It was his responsibility to care for her, not some stranger off the street. If that was inconvenient at times ... too bad.

John stood. Katie recognized the look in his eyes. There was no sense in arguing. They were going home.

John's nerves were raw, and the drive home seemed interminable. His stomach churned with a growing belief that leaving Maggie alone with Laura had been a tremendous mistake. Maggie was frightened. He knew it. He could feel it. There wasn't a doubt in his mind.

~

Knowing how important it was to maintain eye contact with a patient suffering from dementia, Laura knelt by Maggie's side. "Hi Maggie. Do you remember me? I'm Laura. Will you come into the bathroom with me?"

Maggie looked at her and smiled. Laura, she thought, that's a pretty name. It's time to wash up. Maggie held out her hand and stood.

Laura took her hand and guided Maggie to the bathroom. Laura examined the bathroom with a trained eye and made a mental list of suggestions for John. The bathroom can be a dangerous place for Alzheimer's patients, especially as their self-care abilities decreased. It would be a good idea to install grab bars in the tub and a shower chair wouldn't hurt either.

"How about a nice bubble bath Maggie?" Laura asked as she started the water, carefully checking the temperature. She added the scented bath foam she found on the shelf. It might be a good idea to tell John to turn down the temperature on the hot water heater. That would reduce the risk of Maggie scalding herself if she were to try to run the water herself.

Maggie watched, fascinated by the growing mountain of bubbles.

Satisfied, that the water was a comfortable and a safe temperature, Laura turned her attention back to Maggie. Now comes the hard part, she thought. "Okay Maggie, it's time to get undressed for your bath." She gently lowered Maggie's robe from her shoulders. Maggie stood quietly and smiled. So far; so good.

"Good job. Can you unbutton your pajama top?"

Maggie glanced down at her flannel pajamas and then glared at Laura. "No."

Making sure to keep her voice calm and the words slow and clear, Laura began to speak. "Okay Maggie. I am going to reach out and unbutton your shirt. We have to take it off so you can take a bubble bath. You want to take a bubble bath, don't you?"

Maggie nodded. She liked bubble baths.

Laura slowly unbuttoned the first button. "Okay, we have the first one, only a few more to go." She held her breath and slowly unfastened the remaining buttons, making sure to describe each movement as she went. Finally, the task was completed and she began to slip the shirt from Maggie's shoulders.

Maggie's eyes widened in shock and horror. She clutched her shirt and creamed. "No! John! I want John!"

Laura sighed. She should have known things were going way too smoothly. "Maggie, look at me." She paused to make sure she had Maggie's attention. "John isn't here. He asked me to help you with your bath. Remember me? I'm Laura. I am your friend."

"Friend." Maggie repeated.

Laura smiled. "That's right. I am your friend. Now, we have to take your shirt off so you can take a bath. Just look at those bubbles. Don't they look nice?"

Maggie looked at the bath and smiled. "Bubbles."

"Okay, I'm going to take your shirt off now." Laura slowly slid one shoulder down. "That's good Maggie. You are doing a good job."

Maggie shuddered and howled like a wounded animal. Her eyes flashed wildly as panic consumed her. She slapped Laura away and grabbed a hairbrush from the vanity. Before Laura had a chance to protect herself, Maggie swung the brush and connected soundly with Laura's left eye.

Shocked, Laura instinctively covered her face as she stood helpless against Maggie's delirious attack.

Maggie was hysterical and completely out of control. A blood-curdling scream rose from the deepest part of her gut as she flailed her arms at Laura, her nails digging into her exposed flesh.

Laura struggled to remain calm as she slowly backed out of the bathroom that had suddenly become a war zone.

~

John slammed the car into park. He and Katie jumped out of the car and ran to the front door. John's hands were sweaty and trembling as he fumbled with the key to the lock. Finally, the door swung open and their ears were immediately assaulted by the sound of Maggie's hysterical screams. John's stomach lurched as they ran to the source of the sound.

Ignoring Laura, John rushed to Maggie's side. She turned on him with a frenzied madness. Her screams intensified as she pounded her fists on his chest. John was shocked and horrified by the ferocity of Maggie's attack. Clearly, his presence only fueled Maggie's fire. Reluctantly, he stepped aside.

"Katie, will you try to calm your mother down? Apparently, I'm not the person for the job." He was angry and sick to his stomach with guilt. Why didn't he listen to his inner voice in the first place? He never should have left Maggie with a stranger.

After a shock filled moment, John finally noticed Laura. Scratch marks marred her complexion and the beginnings of a nice shiner shadowed her left eye. John cupped her elbow and lead her into the den. He did his best to hold his anger at check. It wasn't fair to cast blame on Laura before he heard her side of the story. Besides, it looked like Maggie had really did a number on her. He poured two snifters of brandy and handed one to Laura.

"I think we both could use a drink. Now, do you mind telling me what the hell happened here?" John demanded, his voice harsher than he intended.

Laura sipped the brandy. She wasn't much of a drinker, but it was just what she needed at the moment. "I really don't know. Everything seemed fine after you left. I took Maggie into the bathroom to take a bath. She was in good spirits and fairly cooperative at first, but as soon as I tried to help her get undressed, she went totally berserk. I did my best to try to calm her down, but there was no stopping her. Thank God you came home when you did."

Relaxed from the brandy, her tears began to fall. She felt awful. Never, in all of her years of caring for patients had anything like this ever happened.

John nervously cleared his throat. Laura's pitiful whimpers made him uncomfortable. He could hardly be angry at her when she had suffered such brutal injuries at the hands of his mild mannered wife. He squelched the urge to smile. While his heart went out to Laura, she certainly didn't deserve to be mistreated this way, he couldn't suppress a certain amount of pride in Maggie. She couldn't be held accountable for her actions. Clearly, she felt threatened and did what she needed to do to protect herself. If nothing else, she could still defend herself.

"John, I hope you'll understand, but under these circumstances, I don't think I am the right person for this job." Laura finished her brandy and smiled meekly. It was the understatement of the century.

John nodded. He stood and extended his hand. "No offense, but I couldn't agree more. I'm sorry this happened, and I will make sure you are fairly compensated for your injuries."

"Thanks. I can't tell you how sorry I am about this. I swear nothing like this has ever happened to me before. I'm sure you will be able to find someone else that can work well with Maggie. I guess we just weren't a good match. Now, if it's okay with you, I'll sneak out the front door. I don't want to upset Maggie again. It sounds like Katie has her under control."

John noticed the blissful sound of silence. Yes, it seemed that at least the screaming had stopped. Thank God for Katie. "Yes, I think you may be right."

John escorted Laura out the door and collapsed against it. Thank God, the worst was over. He found Katie and Maggie, sitting in the kitchen, sharing milk and cookies. John poured himself a glass of milk and joined them

Maggie stared at John and frowned. His guilt grew...

38

No one ever promised me a rose garden, but I was hoping for more than weeds. My days and nights are difficult, but never boring. Sometimes I wonder who is more confused, Maggie or me. Maggie's realm of reality seems to have shifted to the past. I never know who I will wake up with in the morning. Some days, she is a young child and she thinks I am her father. On other days, she is the young mother of Katie and Michael. She has adopted two old teddy bears as surrogates for her babies. It is like living with a cast of characters from a bad sitcom or soap opera.

It is obvious that she doesn't always recognize me as her husband. Thankfully, she seems to realize I am someone that she knows and trusts. Regardless, this is terribly hard to accept. Sometimes, she talks about me, but her memories are all about a much younger man. Star Trek has nothing on me. I almost believe I am living in a time warp. "Beam me up Scottie."

Dr. Hardy and Dr. Mason tried to warn me about this. I knew the day would come and I tried to prepare myself for it, but it was impossible. I'll never forget the first time she gazed at me with that blank look on her face. I knew our present life had slipped away, and it broke my heart.

It is impossible to describe the horrors of this nightmare. It can't be real. How can it be possible? You wake up one morning and the person you have loved for over forty years, suddenly no longer knows who you are. How do you begin to prepare yourself for that? I don't think you can.

I try desperately to find some bright spots in this tragedy, but let me tell you, they are far and few between. At least she is more cooperative with bathing and daily cares, but that could change tomorrow. For now, she does well at following simple instructions, as long as you give them to her one at a time. It is a painfully slow process just to get her dressed for the day, but it is a huge improvement over the fighting.

I am learning. Experience has taught me that on the days she doesn't want to cooperate, it is better to leave it alone. Believe me, a dirty Maggie in her pajamas is much easier to live with than an unhappy clean one.

If I had to choose what part of this process is the most difficult, I would have to say the days when she is troubled or scared are the most taxing. Sometimes, she is a young girl waiting for her parents to come home. She will sit and wait for them for hours. I've seen her work herself into a frenzy worrying about them, because of course, they never come.

I've listened to the doctors, and I have read the books, but this has really been a period of learning by trial and error to deal with this behavior. In the beginning, when this phenomena of living in the past first manifested itself, I tried a method the experts call Reality Orientation. It is designed to bring the patient back to the present. Seems like a good idea, right?

The process goes something like this: Whenever Maggie drifted into the past, I would calmly explain to her that she was a sixty-eight year old woman with grown children of her own. Her parents were never coming home.

It was a horrible experience for the both of us. She was seldom totally convinced I was telling the truth, and besides that, she would relive the grief of losing her parents over and over again. Perhaps it is a successful tool in some cases, but it seems terribly cruel to me.

It is a constant struggle that I find exhausting. Usually, I just play along, unless she is upset by a memory. Sometimes I can simply divert her attention by offering a new activity. I feel blessed when this works, because it is pure hell when it doesn't. Let's just say, when Maggie ain't happy, ain't nobody happy.

I doubt I will ever find a way to adequately thank Dr. Hardy for everything he has done for us (except by paying his bill). Taking Maggie anywhere is a nightmare, but doctor appointments were beyond description. Perhaps he just hated to see his waiting room disrupted by our presence, but whatever the reason, he offered to come to our house. Can you imagine, a doctor that still makes house calls? Unbelievable. I relish his words of encouragement. He says he is impressed by the way we have managed Maggie's care. Despite her cognitive decline, she is still in very good physical condition.

Katie, Craig and Michael have been a Godsend. No child, whatever their age, should have to suffer through this grueling journey. Yet, they unfailingly set aside their own grief, roll up their sleeves, and dive into the often horrific world of Alzheimer's. Without their help and support, I would have had to place Maggie in a nursing home months ago. I've finally realized I'm not Superman, despite my heroic efforts.

Michael comes home as often as he can, and I must admit it is awfully nice to have a doctor in the family, although I imagine it is quite an emotional burden for him. He has offered to take an extended leave of absence so he can come home to help on a more permanent basis. I am touched by his offer, and I admit to being tempted, but I have encouraged him to put off that decision for a while. I may need his help more, later on.

I can imagine that it is very difficult for him to be so far away from the family right now. We are all victims of our own guilt. But for now, he has other patients that need him.

John

39

Now that school is out for the summer, Jacob comes over nearly every day. At first, I worried that he was spending too much time here. I thought he should be spending more time with kids his own age. However, after watching him and Maggie interact together, I believe this experience will be a lifetime treasure for him.

It doesn't seem to bother him that Maggie doesn't always know who he is. Sometimes she calls him Michael and he just giggles. Maggie responds wonderfully to him. They play Monopoly for hours on end. Of course, there are no rules to the game, but it doesn't matter. They simply enjoy each other's company.

I envy him.

John

~

Step on a crack,
Break your mother's back.
Step on a spine,
Break your father's spine.

"What a beautiful day. Mom really seems to enjoy the fresh air." Katie said to John as they strolled the sidewalk with Maggie and Jacob leading the way.

"She does, and after being cooped up all winter long, I must admit I feel a tad bit like a prison inmate let out on parole. It's great to be out of the house. Besides, Maggie needs a little exercise."

"Hey Jacob, slow down. You and grandma are getting too far ahead of us." Katie shouted, and then turned back to John. "Did I tell you that Craig has to go out of town on business next week?"

"No, where is he going?"

Katie laughed. "I don't know, Denver or Detroit, someplace that starts with a D. It doesn't matter; I have it written down at home. The point is, he will be gone and I hate it. You know what happens every time he leaves. The kids get the flu, the car breaks down or the water heater goes to hell."

John chuckled and gently patted Katie's back. "I know. It stinks, but just remember, it could be worse."

Katie winced. "Oh God! I'm sorry, I shouldn't dump this crap on you. You have enough on your plate without me complaining about my petty problems."

"Hey now, don't feel that way. Alzheimer's has definitely thrown us an unwelcome loop, but believe it or nor not, life is not all bad. I have learned a lot about myself, and Maggie, during this time. Besides, I will always be your father and you can cry on my shoulder any time. As your mother would say, it is in the children's owner manual."

John paused and watched Jacob and Maggie for a moment. "What in the world are they doing?"

Jacob and Maggie looked like a couple of drunks, staggering down the sidewalk. The reason soon became clear as the sound of a childhood rhyme reached their ears. "Step on a crack, break your mother's back. Step on a line, break your father's spine."

"Look at Mom. She looks like a school girl. She is really enjoying herself."

"I know. It might sound stupid, but sometimes I actually envy her. Alzheimer's has robbed her of almost all inhibition. She is free to simply enjoy herself. Of course, there is a down side to that too." John chuckled.

"Well, they sure like they are having fun." Katie grinned mischievously. "What do you think?"

John smiled. "If you can't beat 'em, join 'em."

Time disappeared, as the group giant stepped and jumped across cracks in the sidewalk. They squealed in delight when they approached a crumbling sidewalk, badly in need of repair. They met the challenge and deftly ignored the curious looks of bystanders. They played until they were exhausted and returned home.

~

Journal Entry

I suppose today was an ordinary day; if there is such a thing anymore. Maggie was still asleep, (and in bed) when I woke up. Careful not to wake her, I crawled out of bed and tiptoed into the kitchen to treat myself to a peaceful cup of coffee. I can't begin to describe how much I treasure those tranquil moments. Everyday has become a new adventure and I must confess, I don't always feel up to the challenge.

Thank goodness, Maggie has some good days when she is cooperative and social. I treasure those days. Unfortunately, the days that she becomes belligerent and uncommunicative are coming much more frequently. Those times are dreadful. It seems that no matter how hard I try, there isn't anything I can do to make her happy.

Please don't misunderstand me. I am not complaining, well at least not much, nor am I trying to pass any judgment on her. I don't blame her for becoming frustrated and angry. God only knows what I would be like if the situation was reversed. Maggie probably would have given up on me a long time ago, and I wouldn't blame her.

After a heavenly second cup of coffee, I heard Maggie stir. So, I went into the bedroom to wish her a good morning. Sometimes, I can pick up a clue as to how the day will go by her mood in the morning. It doesn't always work, but it helps to be emotionally prepared if possible. Maggie smiled the moment she saw me. Her smile means the world to me.

I picked out her clothes for her. It was an easy choice. There are just a few outfits she likes to wear (It makes me think of her grandmother). We went into the bathroom to wash up and thankfully, Maggie was in great spirits. For some reason, she found the entire process terribly funny. Her laughter was contagious and before I knew it, we were both laughing like a couple of idiots. It was a glorious time.

When Maggie was first diagnosed with Alzheimer's, I believed we would never find anything to laugh about again. But in truth, I have laughed more than I have cried. One has to develop a sense of humor to survive this. If you took everything about this disease to heart, every day would be emotionally crushing.

Maggie was full of energy. She couldn't sit still. She gets like that sometimes. I swear she is wearing a path into the carpet. She spends hours just pacing back and forth through the house. It was one of those days, and I have to admit those marathons really get on my nerves.

I do have a few tricks up my sleeve. For instance, I have a huge laundry basket that I keep full of towels for her to fold. When she is finished with the task, I simply unfold them and repeat the process. If I am lucky, this will keep her busy for a couple of hours at a time. I felt guilty about the deception at first, but I have convinced myself that it helps her feel useful.

So, I brought out the basket, but she had no interest in it. There was nothing I could do to stop the pacing, so I grabbed the newspaper and did my best to ignore her and retain my sanity. Believe me, it isn't an easy task.

John

~

John stood in the doorway and carefully watched Maggie tiptoe her way across the kitchen floor. Initially, he was concerned that she was injured in some way. Every step seemed to be such an effort and her body lurched as she tried to balance herself.

After a few minutes, it finally dawned on him that she was playing the "step on a crack" game. John was amazed that she even remembered it. The game was certainly a challenge on the tiled kitchen floor. It seemed humorous at first, so he watched in quiet wonder.

What was she thinking of? What triggered this memory? He longed to understand, but knew those answers were lost to him forever.

Maggie eyes widened in alarm and her breathing quickened. She struggled to remain upright, as her feet repeatedly missed their mark. She cried out each time a line was breached.

It was no longer a game and there was nothing humorous about it. Maggie was in trouble. John slowly walked towards her and gently reached for her elbow. "Maggie, it's John. Let's go into the living room and I'll bring you a nice glass of orange juice."

He held her firmly by the arm and tried to guide her out of the kitchen and onto the safety of a carpeted floor.

Maggie would have no part of it. She pulled away from him, bound and determined to continue her trek across the kitchen floor. It seemed that she was on a mission and wouldn't be satisfied until she had finished. She howled in agony each time she stepped on a line.

This was no longer a childish game to her. Did she truly believe she was causing pain to her parents? John would never know. He tried everything he could think of to steer her out of the kitchen that suddenly seemed loaded with land mines, but nothing worked. Desperate, and nearly as anxious as Maggie, John finally admitted defeat and called in the big guns. Katie would know what to do.

By the time Katie arrived, Maggie was frantic. It was a vicious cycle. The more upset Maggie became, the more lines she stepped on. It was a horrifying spectacle and John was totally helpless to stop it.

"Oh my God. I thought you were exaggerating when you called. When did this start?" Katie asked. This was much worse than she had expected. How did a harmless childish game turn into such a nightmare?

She contemplated her options and an idea hit her. "Stay here and watch her. I'll be right back."

Katie returned to the kitchen with her arms laden with throw rugs that she had collected from every room in the house. "I'm not sure this will work, but it is worth a try."

"What are you going to do?" John asked, still not grasping the purpose of the rugs.

Katie slowly walked towards Maggie and carefully laid a rug down in front of her. She stepped back and laid another, continuing the process until there was a safe path out of the kitchen.

It was a brilliantly simple idea and John was embarrassed he hadn't thought of it himself. Without the threatening tiles, it was a piece of cake to lead Maggie out of the kitchen.

"Maybe I should get the kitchen carpeted." John muttered to himself.

40

I used to believe that I was a strong man. Maybe not so much in the physical sense. I was never much of a He-man, but I believed I was emotionally and mentally strong and sound. There was a time in my life that I was foolish enough to believe that I could handle anything that life threw at me. Well, let me tell you, Alzheimer's is a very humbling disease. Now, I wake up wondering how I am going to survive each day. I go to bed at night exhausted and wake each morning feeling the same. I literally have dreams about getting a good nights sleep.

Oh, I know I shouldn't pity myself. When I consider everything that Maggie has gone through, and continues to face, I am ashamed to feel sorry for myself. My problems are small in comparison. I would trade places with her in a heart beat. I would do anything to save her from this damn disease. Yet, I wouldn't want to put her into the position of being my caregiver. This is a no win situation.

Alzheimer's doesn't strike a single victim. It attacks the entire family.

John

~

Journal Entry

Dear Katie and Michael,

How can I ever begin to thank you for joining me on this grim journey? You have been more supportive than I could have dared hope for. I suppose it really shouldn't come as a surprise to me. You are your mother's children after all. She would expect nothing less from you, simply because it is the right thing to do.

The time I have spent at the support group has been a real eye-opener. It is heartbreaking to realize how many other families are combating this disease. Unfortunately, from what I've witnessed, our family seems to be the exception rather than the rule. You wouldn't believe how many families are literally torn apart because of this plague.

Nursing Home placement seems to be the biggest culprit. I can certainly understand how this would be a very emotional debate. I can only hope and pray that if we have to face that kind of life changing decision, we will approach it together, with love and respect for everyone involved. However, I pray we will never be in that position.

I apologize for the times I allow myself a pity party. Katie, I'm afraid you are burdened with the brunt of that. Thank you for lending me your shoulder when I need it. I hope you understand I am just blowing off steam. It has no reflection on my feelings for your mother. She is the love of my life, and will be until the day that I die.

I must admit there are days that I wonder if I am capable of withstanding another moment of Alzheimer's without losing my mind. The repetitive questions and the constant pacing sometimes push me to the brink of my endurance. I find myself frequently taking a deep breath and reminding myself that despite the changes, this stranger I now live with is still my wife and my love.

I want you to know that your mother kept this journal from me for years. If it weren't for Alzheimer's I would probably never learned her little secret. As far as I know, it is the only secret she has successfully kept from me for all of our years together. I remember the day she finally showed it to me. She was so afraid I would think it was silly. How could I think anything she did was silly?

I'll never forget the day we received the diagnosis. It was the most devastating moment in my life. I wasn't well informed about the disease, but I knew enough to know that our live had been changed forever. It was easier to bury my head in the sand and the bottle than to face the truth. I'm afraid I really let your mother down, but it won't happen again.

As I think back now, I am ashamed to admit I wasn't very supportive in the beginning of our journey. In your mother's usual style, she was determined to face this disease head on. She spent hours in the library, studying everything she could get her hands on about Alzheimer's Disease. Instead of supporting her, I did my best to discourage her. I realize now that I simply didn't want to face the truth. I must confess, I was angry at her. That is my greatest shame.

Well, reality has certainly slapped me in the face. The way I see it, I have two basic choices. I can face whatever lies ahead and deal with it, or I can tuck Maggie away in a nursing home and visit her on Sundays. So you can see, I have no choice. I vowed to love her in good times or bad, in sickness and health, and that is what I intend to do.

Allow me to thank you in advance for all the help and support I will no doubt receive from you in the days and months that lay before us. My only hope is that Maggie will be able to live out her remaining time on earth with the peace, love and dignity, that she so richly deserves.

May God bless us all.

Dad

41

John stirred and caught the unmistakable aroma of frying bacon in the air. His stomach growled in response. There was nothing better than the smell of bacon. Certain that he must be dreaming he rolled over, closed his eyes and lulled himself back to sleep.

A blood-curdling scream interrupted his tranquil slumber. He instinctively reached for Maggie and found her side of the bed empty. Stunned and panicked, he bolted upright at the exact moment the smoke alarm began to shriek. Swallowing hard, in a futile effort to force his heart back into his chest, he ran to the kitchen.

It was a scene from his worst nightmare come true. Black smoke was filling the room as flames from a frying pan licked the wall. John rushed to the stove and turned off the burner. Quickly, he reached for the box of baking soda and doused the flame. Satisfied that the fire was totally extinguished, he could safely turn his attention to Maggie.

She was crouched in the corner, holding an obviously badly burned hand to her chest. Terror blazed in her eyes and echoed in her screams. John understood her horror. Fire was Maggie's greatest fear. It was a phobia that had cursed her since her father's death in a foundry accident.

John held out his arms as he slowly approached her. He was desperate to comfort her, but he also needed to get a closer look at her injuries. As he drew near, Maggie turned to run, but there was no escape. She was trapped in the corner. John took a deep breath and made his move. He grabbed her firmly by the shoulder and pulled her toward him.

Maggie growled and hissed, reacting like a wounded animal. Her expression showed no sign of recognition and John doubted she knew who he was. Determined to protect herself, Maggie lashed out with her unwounded hand and raked her nails down John's cheek. He backed up, but her attack continued with a mad frenzy. Her screams pierced his eardrums as her fists pummeled his body.

John stepped back and tried to calmly assess the situation. He had to find a way to quiet Maggie down. She was obviously in a great deal of pain and needed medical attention. Even from a distance it was apparent that her burns needed medical attention.

Pain and fear were an awesome force. Maggie was completely out of control. She started to grab glasses and dishes from the cupboard and threw them to the floor. Nothing was safe from her fury. Glass shattered and shards littered the floor. Maggie's bare feet were being sliced and she was leaving a trail of blood as her dangerous tantrum continued to escalate.

There wasn't a moment to spare. This wasn't a situation John could handle on his own. As much as he hated to leave Maggie unattended for even a moment, he knew he had to get help. He ran to the phone and made the three necessary phone calls. The first was 911, the second to Katie, and a frantic third to Dr. Hardy. By this time, John was as hysterical as Maggie.

It seemed he had barely hung up the phone when Katie and Craig burst through the door. Thank God, the Calvary had arrived. Katie took one look at the disastrous scene in the kitchen and froze dead in her tracks. Maggie was emptying the cupboards with incredible speed and glass exploded on the floor.

Thank God, Craig was able to remain calm enough to take some control of the situation. "John, have you called 911?"

"Yes, right before I called you. I called Dr. Hardy too. He is on his way over." John answered.

"Well, since we are expecting company, I suggest you put on some clothes."

John looked down, surprised to find he was dressed in nothing but his boxer shorts. Clothes had been the last thing on his mind, but he supposed he should put something more appropriate on.

Katie attempted to approach Maggie. Glass crunched beneath her feet. "Mom, I've come to visit you. It looks like you hurt yourself. Can we go into the bathroom so I can get a better look?"

Maggie stopped, still holding a plate in her hand. Tears streaked her face and it was easy to see she was exhausted from her destructive tirade. "Hurt."

Katie stepped closer, almost near enough to touch her. Maggie stood still and seemed resigned to accepting Katie's help. Suddenly, the wail of sirens pierced their ears. Maggie immediately retreated to the safety of her corner. Her howls matched the deafening siren's pitch.

John raced back into the room, still struggling with the sleeve of his shirt as paramedics stormed into the room and rushed to Maggie. Glass crunched under their feet as they crossed the kitchen floor. It seemed like a scene out of a bad movie. The swat team storms the crime scent to capture the bad guy. Unfortunately, this wasn't a movie and Maggie was the victim, not the crook.

Terror gleamed in Maggie's eyes. Fear was palpable in the air. Maggie fought to protect herself from the unknown assailants. God only knew what terrifying thoughts were going through her mind. She struggled valiantly, but her efforts were futile. In there effort to assist her, the paramedics practically tackled her.

"What the hell are you doing? She has Alzheimer's. You can't treat my mother that way." Katie rushed to her mother's defense, trying to pull the men off of Maggie. "What the fuck is the matter with you people? You are hurting her. Stop it!"

"Get away lady. We have a job to do." One of the paramedics gruffly ordered, dismissing Katie without listening to her pleas. "Is she allergic to anything?" He asked.

"No." John mumbled, as he watched the paramedic load a syringe and stab Maggie's arm. "Please be careful. You are frightening her. Maggie has Alzheimer's, she doesn't understand who you are or what you are doing. Please let me or my daughter talk to her."

The paramedic stood up and faced John. "Listen, I need you to stand back and let us do our job. If you can't mind your own business, you will need to leave the room."

John's face turned crimson with fury. "Mind my own business? You listen to me, asshole. Maggie is my business and I won't have you treating her like some kind of an animal. She is hurt and she is confused, but I insist you treat her with the dignity and kindness she deserves."

Thankfully, Dr. Hardy chose that moment to enter the fray. No doubt it was a shocking sight. The kitchen was a disaster zone. Smoke and the smell of burned bacon still lingered in the air. Two hulking men were struggling to restrain a one hundred and ten pound woman in the corner. Maggie was giving them the fight of their lives. Craig was holding Katie as she sobbed helplessly into his chest, and John seemed to be ready to engage in fisticuffs with one of the paramedics. The situation was obviously out of control.

He marched to the corner and grabbed the largest paramedic by the shoulder. "Let go of her now!" His voiced boomed. The paramedic's anger evaporated as he recognized the source of the voice. They released their hold on Maggie and retreated to the center of the room.

Maggie's struggles turned to sobs as John rushed to her side. The sedative started to take affect and she fell silent as John gently lifted her in his arms.

"Take her into the living room. Let's get her out of this mess. I'll be with you in a moment." Dr. Hardy instructed.

He waited until the family was out of earshot before turning to the now very timid paramedics.

"What the hell happened here? Were you aware this woman is an Alzheimer's patient?"

"Well yes, the daughter and the husband mentioned it, but she was totally out of control. We had to restrain her for her own safety." A paramedic answered in their defense.

"Well, let me tell you this. You are all idiots. I don't know where you got your training, but you obviously need a refresher course on Alzheimer's Disease. Granted, your first order of business is to protect the patient, but there was no need to physically attack and emotionally traumatize her. As far as I am concerned, none of you are qualified to administer first-aid to a dog." He pulled out a pen and pad of paper from his pocket. "Tell me your names."

He wrote down the information and dismissed them. "Now, get the hell out of here, but rest assured, you haven't heard the end of this yet. I promise I will be reporting this incident to your superiors."

Maggie finally succumbed to the sedative and her exhausting ordeal, and was sound asleep on the sofa. It was a blessing in disguise as it gave Dr. Hardy the freedom to closely examine and treat her wounds. The burns on her hand and arm were serious, but would heal in time. Thankfully, the cuts on her feet were superficial. They would be painful, but she didn't need any stitches.

After carefully applying ointments and bandages to all of Maggie's injuries, Dr. Hardy stood to address the family. "Under normal circumstances, I would recommend that Maggie be admitted to the hospital. However, after this dreadful ordeal, I'm afraid the strange surroundings would just compound her problems. But, I need to advise you that these injuries are going to require a great deal of treatment. There is a real danger of infection. So, it is really up to you."

"I don't think she should go to the hospital." Katie quickly answered. "I am more than willing to learn how to care for her wounds, but maybe it would be a good idea to ask Michael to come home for awhile."

"I think that would be an excellent idea." Dr. Hardy agreed.

"I'll call him right now." Katie announced, grateful to have something constructive to do.

Satisfied that Maggie would sleep awhile, Dr. Hardy poured a round of stiff drinks. "Doctor's orders." He explained as he handed them out.

John glanced at the clock. It wasn't even noon yet. It felt like days had passed since he had gotten out of bed. Oh well, it was five o'clock somewhere and the drink tasted damn good.

~

Journal Entry

Hopefully, it will help to put this on paper, but I doubt anything is capable of assuaging my guilt. How will I ever sleep again? Thank goodness Maggie will be okay. As terrifying as the situation was, it could have been so much worse. Of course, everyone is trying to reassure me that it wasn't my fault, but I know the truth. I let my guard down and now, Maggie suffers.

The kitchen is the least of my worries. A few new dishes and a fresh coat of paint and it will be good as new. If only healing Maggie could be that simple.

I'm doing my best not to harbor any ill will towards the paramedics. There is no denying, their approach to the situation was ignorant, but sadly their attitudes aren't isolated. Dementia is greatly misunderstood. Unfortunately, many victims of dementia are judged as "crazy" and deemed dangerous. There is a huge difference between dementia and mental illness.

Still, I was happy to hear from Dr. Hardy that they were reprimanded for their actions.

It is a small solace.

John

42

Dear Michael,

Once again, I am in your debt. I am eternally grateful for everything you have done for your mother and myself these past few weeks. It is a huge relief to see Maggie's wounds heal, at least the physical ones. The scars on her hand and arm will forever fuel my guilt. They will be a constant reminder of my negligence. I will never forgive myself.

This is the first time I have had the opportunity to witness your skills as a doctor. You are without a doubt, a very caring and capable physician. I am very proud of you. I am just terribly sorry that your latest patient was your mother.

Lord knows, she was a far cry from being a model patient. She fought you during every dressing change. I never would have been able to handle it on my own. You never showed it, but it must have broken your heart to see your mother react in that way. Yet, you never faltered. You never regressed from the role of a doctor, caring for his patient. But the fact remains, you were still a son trying to cope with the impossible behavior of his mother. Despite your outward calm and professionalism, it had to affect you.

I also want to thank you for the generous offer to extend your leave of absence indefinitely to help with your mother's care. It wasn't an easy offer to refuse. The thought of being alone again is terrifying.

Although I will certainly miss your help with Maggie's day to day care, I think I will miss your companionship most of all. I will treasure the memories of our late night conversations for the rest of my life. It was a real pleasure to relax, share a drink or two and have a real adult conversation. It is such a simple thing, but it seemed like a gift from God. It was a true joy to discuss news, politics and sports with someone who not only understood the topics, but was able to respond intelligently to the conversation. I have had such limited contact with the outside world these past few months that I almost forgot there was life beyond Alzheimer's Disease. Perhaps I should consider going to the support group again, or would that still be limiting my circle?

In a funny sort of way, this experience has helped me understand some of your mother's frustrations when you and Katie were young. She didn't complain frequently, but there were times when she felt she would go insane if she didn't have some kind of meaningful contact with another adult besides me. Apparently, I wasn't always the best company. I can certainly sympathize with those feelings now. There are definite similarities between her situation and mine, except for one sad difference. While she was dealing with two young children, I am caring for an adult who is now reduced to the emotional capabilities of a child.

I hope I don't sound bitter. I try not to, but sometimes it seems impossible to maintain a positive attitude. It was easier when you were here. It was nice to share a laugh or two. Now, that I am alone, everything seems terribly sad. There isn't a bright light at the end of the tunnel, just constant reminders of everything we have lost. I miss your mother so much.

Sometimes, I will find her sitting quietly in a chair and it seems so normal, I can almost convince myself that everything is fine. Sadly, the illusion is always destroyed and the nightmare resumes.

I remember when we were first diagnosed; Maggie said she wished it would have been cancer. I thought she was out of her mind at the time, but now I almost agree with her. I hope that doesn't sound uncaring. I just can't imagine anything else being as cruel as this disease.

Your mother wanted nothing more than to be remembered. It seemed like such a simple request. How could she ever be forgotten? Yet, that person seems so far away now. Sometimes it is a struggle to remember how things used to be. We have all changed, and we will never be the same again.

Forgive my ramblings. I wrote this to thank you, and so I will.

Thank you for being Maggie's son. I can't think of higher praise to give anyone.

Love always,

Dad

~

Journal Entry

Praise the Lord, I made it through another day. That seems to be my only criteria for success these days. I'll never know if the trauma of the burn caused this drastic change in Maggie, or if it would have happened anyway. I've asked Dr. Hardy about it, but as usual, he was unable to give me any answers. Why do I bother asking the questions? No one knows shit about this disease.

I barely recognize Maggie anymore. I don't recognize my own house anymore. Hell, I'm not sure who I am anymore. Do I sound bitter? Damn right!

Once Maggie's injuries healed, she was up and running and she hasn't stopped since. It is like living with a wild tornado. Katie and Craig came over a couple of days ago and helped me pack up everything that wasn't nailed down or too heavy to move. Nothing in the house is safe or sacred. If Maggie can pick it up, she can throw it.

Half of the knickknacks she has so lovingly collected through the years are nothing more than forgotten rubble. I used to hate all of the clutter she brought home. I teased her unmercifully about all of her dust collectors. Now, my heart breaks a little with each piece she destroys.

Not only did we have to clear away the breakables, we had to Maggie proof the entire house. We put childproof locks on all of the kitchen cupboards and drawers. The last thing I need is for her to get a hold of a knife. Needless to say, our dishes are all made of plastic these days.

She isn't only angry; she is completely paranoid. She is convinced I am trying to poison her. It is nearly impossible to get her to eat anything. It's hard to imagine that she is able to sustain this thought process, but she does. She examines everything I prepare for her with total suspicion. I thought things were getting better the other day. I left her alone to eat her lunch and when I returned her plate was empty. Unfortunately, it was just wishful thinking. I found her sandwich stuffed into her pocket when I put her to bed that night. I sure wish I hadn't made egg salad.

She barely talks anymore, but when she does, it is the language of a seasoned sailor. It's very difficult to hear that kind of language coming out of the mouth of a lady who rarely cursed. I wasn't even aware she was familiar with that kind of profanity.

Dr. Hardy tells me that if her weight doesn't stabilize soon, he will have no choice but to admit her into the hospital. Of course, I don't want to see that happen. I just don't know how to convince her to eat. I must do something. I'm terrified of the prospect of her being admitted to the hospital. I can't get Frank and Nancy out of my mind. There is no sense in giving history a chance to repeat itself.

Secretly, there is a part of me that almost wishes that Dr. Hardy would take the decision out of my hands. Of course, I remember my promise to always take care of her, but I have almost reached my breaking point. How long can I continue like this? I realize I am no longer a young man, but I feel so much older than my years. God help me. I am tired, so tired.

Lord knows, I'm not alone. The kids are great. Katie comes over every single day and Michael comes home every chance he gets. But, it doesn't take an Einstein to see the toll this has taken on them too. How long can I justify compromising everyone's health and happiness for the sake of one person?

Forever?

John

43

<u>Journal Entry</u>

    I have never considered myself to be a prude. Although I've never been a fan of Playboy or X-rated movies, I've never condemned those who enjoy those avenues of entertainment. However, I find myself completely shocked and unsure as to how to handle this current situation.

    This morning, I found Maggie lying naked on the sofa, frantically involved in the activity of pleasing herself. Logically, I know this is a normal part of life, but in all of our years together, I have never known Maggie to masturbate. Perhaps I have been naive. We used to have a very active and fulfilling intimate life together. I never dreamed this was anything she ever thought of, much less engaged in.

    Shocked beyond belief, I called out her name, but she was oblivious to me. My first instinct was to cover her up and stop her. Thankfully, I realized I was only reacting to my own embarrassment. Trying to set aside my own emotions, I tried to assess the situation logically. Alzheimer's had robbed Maggie of all her normal inhibitions. Therefore, she wasn't doing anything wrong. However, my heart wasn't buying it. The sight of my sweet innocent wife, engaging in such wanton behavior on my sofa, was just plain wrong.

    Finally, I decided it was best to leave her alone. She wasn't endangering herself, and it was hard to predict how she might react if I tried to stop her. I had been a witness and a victim of enough of her anger to avoid provoking it.

Feeling like a sick pervert watching her, I left the room and went to the kitchen for a cup of coffee, although a bourbon sounded more tempting at the time. I was foolish enough to think I was prepared for anything that Alzheimer's might throw at me, but this really took me on an unexpected ride. But, in reality, this was more my problem than hers.

The incident brought up memories of the last intimate night we shared. What a disaster that ended up being. I was wracked with guilt and Maggie was left feeling sad and confused. I never intended to hurt her. She is the love of my life and always will be. I never approached her sexually again, not that I didn't want to. It just seemed wrong to think of her in a sexual way.

Now, I can't help but wonder if I have failed Maggie. Perhaps, my fear of taking advantage of her has deprived her of the closeness and tenderness she craves.

I waited awhile and hoping I had given her enough time, I peeked into the living room and found Maggie sleeping like a baby. She looked so sweet and innocent, it was hard to believe it was the same woman a saw just a few minutes ago. I covered her with a blanket and prayed that she would sleep for awhile. I definitely needed some time to get myself together.

The incident left me pretty shook up and worried. Was this a one-time incident, or would it become a new pattern of behavior? Would she try to do it in front of other people? What if she tried to undress in front of the grandchildren?

The logical part of by brain tells me that Alzheimer's is the impetus of this behavior, but my heart wonders. Do I really know

Maggie? I truly believed we had a satisfying life together. Now I have doubts. Did she feel the same?

John

44

It has been eight years since the words Alzheimer's Disease assaulted my ears in Dr. Mason's office. It has been a hell of a ride.

There is very little, if anything left of the woman I love. She has virtually disappeared before my eyes. I miss her with all of my heart and soul. I long to hear the sound of her voice, feel the touch of her hand, and what I wouldn't give to listen to the musical sound of her laughter, just one more time.

Our house is no longer a home. It has taken on the appearance and antiseptic smell of a small hospital. The linen closet is void of our favorite five-hundred count sheets. They are replaced by adult sized diapers, rubber sheets and bedpans. Our King sized bed has been moved to the garage for storage. Maggie has her own hospital bed and I have a small twin size next to her. They are all constant reminders of how much she has failed... And how much we have lost.

Sometimes I think Alzheimer's is simply the reversal of the aging process. The patient starts the process as a full grown functioning adult. Slowly but surely, memories and abilities are stolen from them, until they are almost childlike again. However, it doesn't stop there. It doesn't only rob the patient of his mind; it also rips away your physical abilities. Before long, the patient is reduced to wearing diapers and eating baby food for nourishment. Could anything be worse?

I have tried to reacquaint myself with some of my old friends, but it hasn't been a very successful endeavor. I'm afraid we don't have much in common any longer. I suppose I can't blame them. They have been able to blissfully continue with their lives and golf games, while I have been fighting the battle of the century. Conversations are difficult. They don't know what to say to me and I certainly have nothing in common with them. I can't blame them for not wanting to hear a play by play account of my last eight years with Alzheimer's. Unfortunately, it's the only thing I know. I have been out of the loop too long.

I'm sure I make a lot of our old friends uncomfortable. Perhaps they feel guilty for not being more supportive. I wish I could find a way to reassure them that it isn't their fault. Maggie and I decided early on that we wanted to keep this a private matter. I'm certain many of our good and caring friends would have been there for us, if we had allowed them. I regret that decision now.

It's easy to get depressed. Yet, I suppose there are some things I should be grateful for, but I'm not. Maggie is no longer capable of any episodes of violence or other disturbing activities. I never thought I would say it, but I would give anything to have her pacing around the house again. At least she still had some spunk. Now, she spends hours at a time, simply staring into space. I pray she is in a happy place.

I am blessed with such a wonderful family. Katie is my rock. Although there are times I'm afraid she is spreading herself a little too thin. She spends endless hours here, caring for her mother and helping me keep the household running. It is exhausting work, both physically and mentally, and she still has her own family to care for. But, I realize that there is nothing on earth that could keep her away from her mother during this tragic time.

Lonnie and Marcia come over occasionally, but their visits are infrequent and short. At this point, I can't blame them. Maggie doesn't recognize them anymore. My sympathies really lay with Jacob. His dedication to Maggie has never faltered. He still visits several times a week and spends hours by her side. He talks to her about school and his friends, or sometimes he reads to her. He is an amazing young man. Given his caring nature, we might have another doctor in the family.

And what can I say about Michael? We visit every night by phone and he comes home as often as he can. He helps me cling to my remaining sanity. It won't be long and I may be forced to accept his offer to return home. I need him.

Sometimes, I try to imagine what life will be like when Maggie is gone. It is an unwelcome thought that I am forced to face. Alzheimer's is a terminal disease. That is the ugly fact and there is no escaping it. Sadly, every day brings us closer to that grim reality.

Maggie accepted the promise of death the moment she was diagnosed. Death didn't scare her. She just didn't want to survive long enough to be in the condition she is now. This was her greatest fear.

But, what am I to do? I can't pray for her demise. As long and difficult as our days are, I can't imagine a life without her. I love her. John

45

I am terribly ashamed of myself, but I am definitely paying the price for it. I haven't suffered from a hangover of this magnitude since college. I am smart enough to know that booze isn't the answer, but it seemed a good escape last night.

Michael drove down late yesterday afternoon. He is only able to stay a day or two until he can make arrangements for another leave of absence. Poor guy, we've managed to completely eat up all of his vacation time. We stayed up pretty late last night and I'm afraid our first drink led to too many.

I am no fool, at least most of the time. There are some important decisions that need to be made. Now that Maggie is no longer able to walk or stand by herself, it is very difficult for me to care for her alone. She has become so frail, I'm afraid to transfer her. And she rarely speaks. Yet, I'm able to see past that. I can still see the woman I fell in love with. I know she is in there somewhere.

The kids think it is time to consider nursing home placement. It is impossible to predict how long Maggie may linger in this condition. It might be a matter of weeks or months, but it could also be years. I know they are worried about me, and Michael gently pointed out that I have the right to a life beyond bedpans. I suppose he is right, but it feels wrong. I am foolish enough to believe there is still time for a miracle.

Morning came and regardless of an aching head and a severe case of cottonmouth, Maggie still required my attention. It was time to start the day. I sat Maggie on the edge of the bed and fastened the transfer belt around her waist. She seemed so tiny, I shuddered to think how easy it would be to break her ribs. I lifted gently and transferred her to the commode.

Maggie looked at me and smiled. And then, so very slowly, she raised her hand and gently patted my cheek. Her simple touch was enough to send me over the edge. I fell to my knees and bawled like a baby.

Michael found me with my head buried in Maggie's lap, while she gently ran her fingers through my hair.

John

46

It has been a painful week. Michael and I have been touring nursing homes. We toured one that supposedly has an Alzheimer's Unit that is rated as one of the best in the State. There was very little that impressed me. It was little more than controlled chaos, and not very well controlled at that. Residents wandered up and down the hall, wearing mismatched clothes, looking more like homeless people than patients in a nursing home.

Mrs. Johnson, the social worker, lead us into the day room. It was a depressing sight. A row of recliners sat in front of a droning television, filled to capacity, with residents laying prone, staring blankly into space.

Despite my misgivings, and there were many, the kids agreed that this was the best placement for Maggie. Michael explained our situation to Mrs. Johnson. She seemed understanding and sympathetic enough, but this was obviously old hat to her. She had heard our story a thousand times before. Maggie was just another case to her.

But, she wasn't like these "other people", Maggie was special. She didn't deserve to be tucked out of sight, simply because she was too much work. Guilt weighed heavy in my heart, but I kept my mouth shut. I had been outvoted.

Mrs. Johnson handed Michael a thick stack of paper to read and sign. She encouraged us to get everything back to her as soon as possible so Maggie could be placed on the waiting list.

I couldn't believe my ears. There was a waiting list to get into this place? I was under the impression that things would happen more quickly.

Mrs. Johnson explained that they were currently filled to capacity. Vacancies were not filled on a first come first served basis. There were several people that were on a priority list because they were classified as high risk related to volatile behavior that could result in injury to themselves or others. (Very reassuring to think that Maggie would be locked in a unit with a bunch of mad men.) There wasn't any way to predict how long it may take before they had an appropriate opening for Maggie.

In other words, people had to die first.

Well, I was ecstatic. (Not at the prospect of other people's death, let them live forever.) I had severe doubts about this decision. The delay was a welcome reprieve.

John

47

Dearest Maggie,

It has been a little over two months since we have put you on the waiting list for the nursing home. Mrs. Johnson called me Monday with the good news. They have an appropriate opening for you. I knew this moment would eventually come, but I have been dreading it with all my heart and soul.

Today is your moving day. Your bags are packed and waiting by the door. The nursing home has a specially equipped van that can accommodate your wheelchair. They are scheduled to pick you up at two o'clock this afternoon.

Everyone is here for "The Big Day". I left them sitting in the living room. No one is talking and I couldn't tolerate the roaring silence for another minute. The only sound in the house seems to be the eternal ticking of the clock that just brings me closer to the time they will come to take you away from me.

I wish I could talk to you. I want to beg your forgiveness. But you are sleeping, so I escaped to the den to compose this letter.

Of course, the kids are suffering too. They love you so much and only want to do the "right" thing. I don't doubt their good intentions, but they don't understand what is in my heart. This is an impossible situation for me. Maggie, you are my life, my reason for living. How can I allow them to take you away?

We have shared so many dreams together. Despite Alzheimer's, we have been very fortunate. We have had so many joyous years together. But it isn't enough. The lyrics to "Leaving on a Jet Plane" are playing in my mind. I remember how much you loved that song. It has taken on a whole new meaning today.

This is wrong. I made a promise to you and I intend to keep it. Although the thought of losing you is unbearable, the fear of receiving "the phone call" in the middle of the night is worse. I can't bear the thought of your passing without being at your side.

I don't give a damn what Katie or Michael have to say. You are my wife and I can't and won't let you go. They can either stand by us, or get on with their lives. Frankly, it doesn't matter. You ain't goin' nowhere.

There isn't a person alive, or a power on earth that can take you away from me. Only God has that power, and until he decides to call you home, you will stay by my side.

John

~

Journal Entry

To their credit, the kids handled my decision better than I expected. It goes without saying, they have concerns (so do I), but deep down, I think they are relieved. Perhaps they finally understand that I "need" to care for my lady.

Unfortunately, Mrs. Johnson wasn't nearly as understanding. I realize I only gave her a few hours notice of our change of plans, but I have never been a part to such a rude encounter. She did everything in her power to make me change my mind. Her attitude just strengthened my position. Maggie didn't belong there. Besides, I am hardly leaving her in a lurch, if there is such a long waiting list, there must be another family out there, eagerly waiting for her call. Truthfully, this really saved everyone a lot of grief. Because, if I had gone through with the admission, I would have brought her home before bedtime. Now, that would have been a real mess.

Once the decision was made, we needed to decide how to live with it. Michael made it clear that he was staying home indefinitely. And it goes without saying that Katie will continue to come every day. Thank goodness Craig is so understanding. He agreed wholeheartedly, knowing full well that most of his home chores and childcare would be dumped on his shoulders. He is a good man and Katie is lucky to have him. Let me rephrase that. They are lucky to have each other.

The next step was to call Dr. Hardy. We needed to apprise him of our change of plans. He didn't seem a bit surprised, but I think I detected a note of concern in his voice. I don't blame him. I have concerns of my own.

We unpacked Maggie's bags and did a quick inventory of our supplies. Since we thought Maggie was going to be admitted, we had kept everything to a minimum, so a shopping trip was definitely in order. We worked like a team and there was excitement in the air as we made our lists and developed our plan. It probably sounds odd, but it felt as though we were about to embark on a great adventure. I realize it sounds ridiculous. There was no cause for celebration. We were all too aware of how this particular adventure would end. But, the important thing was we were doing it together. We would face it together...to the bitter end.

Everyone should have a doctor in the family. Michael thought of many things we needed that Katie and I surely would have overlooked. Of course, it is a huge advantage in managing Maggie's every day cares. Michael is able to monitor Maggie's condition very closely. It is probably the greatest advantage we have over other families that are struggling with the home care versus nursing home placement dilemma.

Katie and Craig volunteered to go the pharmacy to pick up our supplies. Michael poured us a drink and we shared a quick toast to Maggie, who was sleeping peacefully in the bedroom. It was where she belonged.

Since we were alone, I mustered up the courage to ask him for his honest opinion about my decision. In his usual diplomatic manner, he said he didn't believe it was a black or white matter. There simply wasn't a right or a wrong. However, he did say that he still believed nursing home placement still had its advantages, but that was because he was concerned about my health.

Then, he flashed me a quick wink and I knew in my heart, I had made the right decision.

John

48

<u>*Journal Entry*</u>

Today is Maggie's birthday. She is only seventy years old. That is young by today's standards. These are supposed to be her golden years. What a joke that is! Of course, the kids came over, but there was very little to celebrate. The Maggie we knew and loved is essentially gone.

Katie dressed Maggie in her prettiest dress, applied her make-up and sprayed her with her favorite cologne. It was a wonderful gesture, but in reality, it just accentuated her drastic decline. The dress hung on her emaciated frame like a tent and the make-up emphasized her gaunt features. Her once sparkling eyes are now sunken and almost lifeless. Her nose and cheekbones are too prominent, and her mouth remains chronically open, like a baby bird waiting to be fed.

This has been a difficult ride for the grandchildren, but they have managed to survive it very well. Lonnie is twenty-three years old now and is in his fourth year of college. He has grown into a fine young man. Maggie would be very proud of him. His goal is to become a doctor, but he plans on specializing in research, Alzheimer's in particular. Who knows, someday he might be instrumental in curing this damn disease. Perhaps he can save other families from this heartbreak. Wouldn't that be something?

Marcia just turned twenty-one and considering joining the Peace Corp. The girl that hated doing her homework was Valedictorian of her High School class. She worked on her speech for weeks and managed to keep it a secret from all of us until the night of her graduation.

Her speech was about "Courage". She spoke of the courage required to leave the safety of high school and begin the trek into the great unknown, be it college or the work force. Change is never easy, but she was unafraid because her grandmother taught her what courage was all about. She stood proudly and described Maggie's fight with the greatest unknown of all...Alzheimer's Disease. She knew in her heart, if her grandmother could face this deadly disease head on, knowing that despite her best efforts, she was destined to fail, then there was nothing on God's green earth that could ever intimidate her. She vowed to carry Maggie's memory with her, as a medal of valor. It was all the motivation she needed to succeed in everything she faced in the future.

Her speech ended with a standing ovation and thundering applause. Needless to say, we were all a bucket of tears. It was one of the high points of my life. It was a shame Maggie couldn't be there.

Jacob is now twelve years old. Dear sweet Jacob. It saddens me to think that he will probably have no real memory of his grandmother prior to Alzheimer's. He has always been Maggie's strongest medicine. Except for a brief period of time when Maggie's behaviors were too extreme for him to handle, he has visited with his grandmother nearly every day. Sometimes I think he has dealt with this situation better than the rest of us. His love is unconditional.

He always greets her with a big hug and kiss. It always reminds me of his very special Christmas gift from years ago. That box is still proudly displayed on our living room. He chats with her by the hour. Perhaps it is my imagination, but Maggie always seems to be more alert during his visits. There are times when I think I can detect a small smile cross her face. It is probably wishful thinking, but it doesn't hurt to dream, does it? I am beginning to believe it is the only thing I have left.

Yes dear Maggie, it is your birthday. Please forgive me if I don't wish you a happy one. I'm sure it is just another day to you. That is, if you are even aware of the passing of time. Every birthday, anniversary and holiday is just another glaring reminder of all we have lost. Time is a precious commodity, and so many memories have been stolen from us. It saddens me to think of everything you have already missed and all that you are bound to miss in the future. You will never see your grandchildren marry. The thrill of bouncing your great-grandchildren on your knee has been stolen from you.

Yet, you will be remembered and your influence will be felt for generations to come. Despite Alzheimer's, or perhaps because of it, you have inspired our grandchildren to become strong individuals who are bound to make a difference in this world.

This journey has changed us all. As painful as these past years have been, I believe we have all grown. Michael believes the experience will make him a better doctor and he is seriously considering specializing in geriatrics. He has always been a caring doctor, but living with Alzheimer's has really opened his eyes to the many difficulties our elderly population has to face when dealing with the health care system. He is thinking about going back to school for nursing home administration. He wants to make a difference. And I have no doubt that he will.

Katie has become very involved in the Alzheimer's Support Group. It really wasn't my cup of tea, but it has been a wonderful experience for her. She helped organize this years Alzheimer's walk. Her efforts were very fruitful. They raised a huge amount of money for Alzheimer's research.

She has also become a strong advocate for other families who are dealing with this nightmare. You would be so proud of her. For someone who used to suffer from severe stage fright, she has become an inspired speaker. She is in constant demand to speak about our experience with Alzheimer's.

Of course, we have always loved Craig. Katie chose her husband well. In Katie's absence, he has taken on carpooling, cooking, cleaning and slumber parties without complaint. He would never admit it, but I know he has sacrificed more than one promotion because it would interfere with his family responsibilities. I know a lot of men who would resent the time Katie spends away from home, despite the reasons, but I have never heard a hint of a complaint from him. He has been a rock, and in many cases, our voice of reason.

And what have I gained from this? I have experienced anger, grief, sorrow, and a pain greater than any soul should ever have to bear. I have prayed to God for a miracle, and I have shaken my fist at that same God.

But, because of you, I have known a love that is timeless. I have learned to relish the feel of grass under my feet, the beauty of a star filled sky, and the simple joy of growing a flower. I have learned the true definition of the word courage. I have learned not to hear, but listen. I have learned the value of family. I have learned not to take tomorrow for granted. Life should be lived to its fullest, every single day.

It dawns on me now that there is cause to celebrate. For without this day, there would be no you.

Yes Maggie, you will be remembered. Your memory will move mountains.

Happy birthday, my darling.

John

49

Michael and Dr. Hardy are trying to get Maggie accepted into a Hospice Program. Hospice care provides care for patients that are in the final phases of an incurable disease. The hospice philosophy recognizes death as the final stage of life. Care is provided for the patient and the family twenty-four hours a day, seven days a week. Hospice care treats the patient rather than the disease, with the goal of allowing the patient to spend their final days in dignity, while also providing emotional support to the family.

It sounds like a wonderful program and I am certain we would all benefit from it. However, it hasn't been an easy process. First, the patient must be diagnosed as terminal to qualify for the program. Logic tells me that Alzheimer's is a terminal disease. There is no hope for Maggie's recovery.

The problem we are facing, is abiding by their definition of terminal. The program requires a doctor's statement certifying that the patient's life expectancy is six months or less. This has been very discomforting. I don't want to put a time frame on Maggie's life. It seems so cold and calculating. Besides that, it is very difficult to predict the life of expectancy of a patient with Alzheimer's. Death could come quickly from pneumonia or some other infection, but they could linger for months or years. There is no way of predicting.

I am a very private person and was hesitant to get involved with a program of any sort. And to be honest, we probably wouldn't have pursued this sort of treatment if it was just a matter of caring for Maggie's daily needs. Unfortunately, it isn't that easy. Bottom line...we need help.

~

Journal Entry

It took a great deal of paper work and perseverance, but Maggie was finally accepted into the program. To qualify for their criteria of being terminal, they used something called the Reisenberg scale. The patient needs to be:

*unable to ambulate without assistance

*unable to dress without assistance

*unable to bathe themselves

*incontinent

*unable to meaningfully communicate

Maggie met their criteria months ago.

Let me be the first to say this was definitely worth the effort. I can't begin to describe what a difference hospice has made in our lives.

Allow me to introduce our health care team. We are provided with several CNA's (certified nursing assistants). But, for the sake of continuity of care, we have a primary CNA who is assigned full-time to our case. Her name is Gloria and she is an angel.

Denise is our Registered Nurse. She visits frequently to monitor Maggie's condition. There seems to be a lot of paperwork involved. It is imperative to maintain very detailed records to remain qualified for hospice services. Denise does her job extremely well, but she is also an extraordinary person. Michael seems very impressed, and I don't believe it is entirely a professional interest.

We are also provided spiritual support. Pastor Tom visits frequently. I've never had a close relationship with a member of the clergy. Although I believe in God, I tend to keep my religious beliefs private. I'm not very comfortable with bible thumpers. However, Tom is different. He offers spiritual support without being too pushy. He doesn't care what religion we are, or how often we go to church. He very simply, cares about us. I already consider him a good friend.

We are all aware that we are quickly approaching the end of our battle. Of course, I can't speak for the rest of my family, but it is an emotionally confusing time for me. I don't want Maggie to die. However, it is incredibly painful to watch her suffer day after day.

Tom has helped me come to terms with some of these extremely painful issues. As heart wrenching as it is, he made me realize it is okay to say good-bye. In fact, it is an important part of the dying process.

Losing someone you love to Alzheimer's is a a profoundly brutal experience. It isn't easy, learning to let go. There are so many difficult decisions to make. I felt as though I was contributing to Maggie's death by signing the Do Not Resuscitate orders. Then, there was the issue of artificial feeding. Would we use a feeding tube in the event that Maggie becomes unable to drink or eat orally. Her daily intake is minimal now, and it is one of my greatest concerns. I don't want her to starve to death.

Michael and Dr. Hardy have both assured me that Maggie would not suffer without the feeding tube. Supposedly, it would be a comfortable way to die. But, how the hell do they know? It was a heartbreaking decision, but I eventually relented to their expertise. Maggie will receive comfort measures only.

Please God, don't let her suffer. I am doing enough for the both of us.

John

50

The Hospice team has become part of our family. How did we survive without them?

It has been especially heartwarming to witness the relationship between Michael and Denise blossom. They did their best to deny their feelings, and maintain a professional distance, but it was a futile attempt at best. Their feelings are bigger than the both of them.

Michael has burdened himself with a lot of unnecessary guilt over the situation. I sympathize with his feelings. I suppose it is natural to feel guilty for falling in love and finding personal happiness while your mother is dying, especially if you fall in love with your mother's hospice nurse.

I've done my best to reassure him. There is no reason to feel guilty. Maggie would never forgive him if he denied himself happiness because of her. Secretly, I believe Maggie has a magic spell emanating from her. Because of knowing her, none of us will ever be the same. Despite our pain and sorrow, she has taught us so much. She has forced us to finally open our eyes to the wonder life is. And now, because of her, Michael has met Denise.

Yes, God does work in mysterious ways. I will never understand him, or totally forgive him. But I know this to be true.
John

~

John opened the front door, surprised to see Pastor Tom on his doorstep. John smiled. Tom was always a welcome guest.

"Come in. Your timing is perfect. Maggie is sleeping and Michael went out for the evening. I was actually feeling a little lonely. It seems I've gotten used to having a house full of people. The quiet was driving me crazy." John paused. "What brings you to my neck of the woods?"

Pastor Tom smiled. "Oh, I was just in the neighborhood and thought I'd stop by." He said as he hung up his coat and made himself to home.

"Okay. What's going on? You look like the cat that ate the canary." John asked.

"Nothing. I just happened to be in the neighborhood and I thought you might like a little company."

"Okay, if you say so. Who am I to doubt the veracity of a member of the clergy? Would you like a drink or something?"

Pastor Tom glanced at his watch. "Umm, not right now. How was Maggie's day?" He asked, eager to change the subject.

Just then, the front door swung open and Michael and Denise appeared, looking like a couple of kids caught with their hands in the proverbial cookie jar.

Michael's hands were filled with two bottles of champagne. He promptly opened one and poured the bubbly into four plastic tumblers. It wasn't the romantic presentation one would normally go for, but since what was left of the good crystal was still packed away, he had little choice.

After passing out the glasses, Michael pulled Denise close and raised his glass. "Dad, Pastor Tom, we would like to make a small announcement."

John smiled. There was no denying the glow of love in their eyes. He raised his glass in anticipation.

Michael cleared his throat as a pink blush reached his cheeks. "I realize Denise and I haven't known each other long, and this may come as a bit of surprise, but we enjoy each other's company and have a lot in common..." He paused briefly to gather his courage. "I guess what I'm trying to say, is that we are deeply and totally in love. We didn't plan it this way, but there is no reason to fight it. Mom has taught us that life is too precious to waste. So, we are getting married."

John's heart swelled with a bittersweet mixture of pride, happiness and sorrow. This was the day Maggie prayed for, and she would never know ... or would she? Moisture filled his eyes as laughter erupted from his mouth. He reached out and hugged Michael and Denise close.

Their embrace was cut short by a knock on the door. Katie and Craig joined the party. The circle of conspirators was now complete. Apparently, John was the only one out of the loop. It was a joyous celebration, yet he felt terribly alone.

Michael offered John a refill of champagne. John declined and decided he needed something a little stronger. Michael followed him into the kitchen, watching him mix his drink.

"You haven't forgotten about your last hangover, have you?" Michael asked with a knowing grin.

"Hell no, but this is worth the risk. Congratulations son. I couldn't be more happy. Denise is a lovely girl. I know you will be very happy together."

"So, you are definitely okay with all of this? I know this is kind of sudden, but I don't want to wait."

John laughed. "Believe me, I understand sudden. Remember, your mother and I got married twenty-seven days after we met."

"Yeah I know, and you guys did okay." He paused for a moment. "I really want Mom at the wedding."

John frowned. "Oh Michael, that is really a sweet thought, but I don't think it is very practical."

Michael smiled. "I know. It would be almost impossible to take her out. That's why I wanted to ask you if it would be okay to have the wedding here at the house. Pastor Tom has already agreed to preside over the ceremony."

John was speechless. It was a beautiful gesture. "Of course, it would be okay. It's a marvelous idea. But, what about Denise? This house isn't exactly the decor most women dream of for their wedding day. Look around." He pointed to the medical equipment that stood in nearly every corner. "It looks more like a hospital than a home, much less a wedding chapel."

"Don't worry about Denise. It was her idea. She loves Maggie too. And as far as the house goes, Katie has already volunteered to take charge of that."

John smiled. "Well, it seems that you've already thought of everything. Let's do it!" He hugged Michael tight.

They joined the others in the living room. Everyone was talking at once. It was an exciting time, but there was a sense of urgency haunting the wedding plans. Maggie's condition was very tenuous. To ensure their wish came true, the wedding had to be soon. And the sooner the better.

The wedding would be held the day after tomorrow.

~

Journal Entry

Dear Maggie,

We are hosting a wedding, and you are the guest of honor. I am so happy for Michael. Denise is a beautiful girl. I know they will be very happy together. Their love is so young and vibrant. Seeing them, brings back so many happy memories. Was it really that long ago that we shared such wondrous feelings?

Pastor Tom is going to perform the wedding ceremony. It is a perfect choice. I'm sure he is happy to preside over such a happy event. It is definitely a nice change of pace from his regular duties.

Darling, I know it is just a matter of time now. The wedding is tomorrow. Please give me one more day.

Love always,

John

51

Well, today is the big day. Michael is as nervous as a cat on a hot tin roof. He hasn't been able to sit still since he got out of bed this morning. I'm not sure what he was more nervous about, getting married or meeting Denise's parents.

They flew into town this morning. Denise picked them up at the airport and brought them to the house to meet us. Doug and Claire are wonderful people. It is easy to see how Denise grew into being such a special woman. If they were surprised by the suddenness of the marriage, they didn't show it.

We visited over Bloody Marys. (Is it just me, or have I been drinking a lot lately?) In a matter of a few minutes, it seemed we had known each other for years. They are a welcome addition to our crazy family. I was especially touched when Michael introduced Doug and Claire to Maggie. I must admit, I was quite apprehensive at first, and sadly a little embarrassed. It didn't seem right to for them to meet her in her current condition. It almost seemed like a betrayal to Maggie. I was tempted to pull out the photo albums and try to describe my "real Maggie", but there wasn't time for that.

Michael took them to her bedside and introduced them. Maggie was awake, but gave no indication that she knew anyone was in the room. As usual, her eyes were open, but unfocused. She was merely staring into space.

To their immense credit, Doug and Claire seemed unfazed by her condition. Without a moment's hesitation or doubt, Claire pulled up a chair and sat by Maggie's side. She reached for Maggie's hand and smiled.

Tears filled my eyes as I eavesdropped on the one sided conversation between the two very special mothers. Claire put into words all of the emotions I knew Maggie would be feeling on her son's wedding day. She spoke of the joy and satisfaction a mother feels when she knows her children are happy. And though they had only met, she was already quite taken with Michael. She looked forward to becoming a family.

It was beautiful and touching, yet the saddest thing I've ever witnessed. Maggie never moved and her blank expression never changed. But I believe, I must believe, that Maggie heard Claire's wonderful words, and agreed.

John

~

Journal Entry

Dear Michael,

The wedding is only a couple of hours away. Katie is going slightly crazy fussing with the flowers and checking on the food. There is enough food to feed a small army. I suppose I shouldn't be surprised. She is her mother's daughter.

Gloria came over early to get Maggie washed and dressed. What did we do without her?

And you my son, are driving me slightly insane. You have been trying to tie your tie for the past two hours. It's hard to believe that you are trained to handle a scalpel.

Since there is very little for me to do other than get in the way, I escaped to the den to write you this letter. Soon, you will be a married man. At the end of a simple ceremony, your life will be changed forever. As I write this, you are probably filled with doubts and wondering what in the world you have gotten yourself into. Well, let me reassure you that all of those doubts will be washed away the moment your beautiful bride walks down the aisle. Well, I guess there isn't really an aisle, but you know what I mean.

It wasn't that long ago that you swore you would never get married. I have to admit, you sounded pretty convincing. However, I always knew that your resolve would crumble when you met the right person. I firmly believe Denise is that woman.

You may find this hard to believe, but I'm not so old that I have forgotten what it feels like to be in love. When I met your mother, the world ceased to spin. My heart ached whenever I was away from her. I know it sounds corny, but we were, and still are, soul mates. We had so much to talk about, we had to get married, just so we could finish our conversation.

Marrying someone twenty-seven days after you meet, brings the critics out of the woodwork. I can't begin to tell you how many people believed we would never make it. Even more surprising, I can't tell you how many people had the courage to voice their negative opinions to my face. Apparently rudeness has no bounds. I hate to say it, but be forewarned. You and Denise will probably face those same skeptics. I don't have a lot of advice in how to handle them, other than to take pride in proving them wrong.

Don't ever hesitate to follow your heart. God only knows where it may lead you. And may he bless you with the joy and happiness your mother and I have shared all of these years. You know, if I were offered a crystal ball on our wedding day, and I was able to peer into the future, it would not have stopped me from standing by her side.

I may have done things differently. I might have spent a little less time at the office. We certainly would have danced a lot more. We might have been less frugal. Believe me, this retirement thing isn't all it's cracked up to be. But, above all else, I would make sure that Maggie knew how deeply I loved her. And I would never take tomorrow for granted, for if there is one thing I've learned from Alzheimer's, it's that you never know what tomorrow might bring.

I have no magic words of wisdom or secrets to a happy marriage. I can only hope that your mother and I have taught you by example to respect each other, love each other, and be each other's best friend.

Thank you for sharing this day with your mother. I suppose some people may claim that it is an empty gesture, designed to soothe your own guilt. Those same ignorant people may say that Maggie won't know the difference. Well, I don't believe that. I believe she is much more aware than we realize. After all, as long as she remains with us, and has breath to breathe, her soul survives. She knows how much we love her, and I know she loves us in return. She is very happy and proud to share this very special day with you and your beautiful bride.

I smile as I imagine how nervous she would be today. Of course, if it weren't for Alzheimer's I doubt we would be holding the ceremony here. I never would have agreed. Your mother would be driving me crazy. Everything would have to be perfect, but in truth, if any one could do it, it would be your mother. She had a creative flair. She could make the mundane magical. Perhaps my memories are seen through rose-colored glasses, but I don't think so.

I know I've said it before, but let me thank you one more time for everything you have done for us these past few months. It can't be easy for a doctor to take such an extended leave from his practice. Although you've never implied this might be a hardship on you, I suspect you may have jeopardized your position at the hospital for us. Perhaps I should have stopped you from staying, (as if I have that kind of power), instead I embraced your offer out of selfishness and fear. I desperately needed your strength and support.

I don't feel too guilty about disrupting everyone's lives. I firmly believe that keeping Maggie at home was the right decision for our family. Ironically, it has been the most painful, yet rewarding time in my life. Bearing witness to Maggie's drastic decline has damned near killed me. Yet, it has brought us so much closer as a family. Of course, it goes without saying, I would give anything to change this ugly chain of events. But if fate had to deal us these cards, I'm glad I played poker with you.

The clock is ticking. Soon, you will be a married man and a new chapter will be opened in your life. I hope God blesses you and Denise with a lifetime of health and happiness. Sadly, the path of life is seldom smooth. Whenever you are faced with trouble, think of your mother, and ask yourself, is this really so bad? Remember her love and courage, and face your troubles head on. As long as you and Denise stand together, nothing will have the power to tear you apart.

I have rambled enough. I suppose I should check to see if you have managed to tie your tie.

God Bless you both,

Dad

52

Journal Entry

Dearest Maggie,

Our son is now a married man. It was your dream come true. It was a beautifully simple ceremony. Pastor Tom did an excellent job. It was a small gathering, but everyone that mattered was here, especially you, my darling.

Michael and Denise are spending their wedding night at a local hotel. It isn't much of a honeymoon, but they didn't want to be too far from home. Katie wanted to stay behind to help clean up, but I told her tomorrow would be soon enough. Truthfully, I wanted the house to ourselves this evening.

Suddenly, I feel so old. Where did all the years go? Wasn't it just yesterday that Katie and Michael were children? You did a wonderful job of guiding them into adulthood. I'm sorry I wasn't more helpful in their early years. I didn't change nearly enough diapers. I'm afraid I was a male chauvinist at heart. I was under the greatly misguided opinion that raising children was women's work. It was my job to bring home the bacon. What a fool I was. I missed so much.

Looking back, I can only pray you knew how much I loved and appreciated you. After your diagnosis, you told me that you wanted no regrets. Yet, I regret so much. I regret the burnt meals because of late nights at the office. I'm sorry that I begged fatigue, rather than take you out on a Saturday night. I'm sorry for not really listening to your troubles. But most of all, I'm sorry for taking you for granted.

I took it for granted that you would always be here by my side. Death or illness never crossed my mind. It was a subject too painful to consider. I was smart enough to realize that I'm not strong enough to lose you. Even now, I can't comprehend a life without you in it.

Sadly, the end is near. I feel it in my soul. There is a hollowness in my heart that could only come from losing you.

I should probably call the kids. But I won't. This night is ours. Tonight you will sleep in our bed, wrapped in my arms.

Good-bye my darling, until we meet again.

Your adoring husband,

John

~

Journal Entry

It is over.

I gently laid Maggie in our bed. She felt so small and frail in my arms, it was like tucking in a small child. We laid together for hours, with only the sound of our breathing to break the silence. Unbearable seconds passed between her breaths. Selfishly, I prayed for each one. Every breath she took was a treasure.

It was too late for miracles. I knew she was leaving. There was nothing I could do, but hold her in my arms and whisper loving words into her ear. I told her good-bye, and reassured her it was okay to leave. It was time for rest. Her job was done. It was the hardest thing I've ever done.

I kissed her forehead, and her eyes fluttered open. Did I imagine it? I don't believe I did. For one brief second there was a clarity to her eyes that I hadn't seen in months.

For that brief moment, time stood still. Maggie knew me, and smiled.

And then she was gone.

EPILOGUE

Michael and I found this journal today. We were cleaning out some of Mom and Dad's things. The journal was tucked away in the infamous Christmas present that Jacob gave Mom so long ago. I'll never forget that day, and apparently Dad felt the same.

Cleaning was quickly forgotten. Michael and I spent the day reading the words written in tattered notebooks and binders. They brought back so many memories and provided a wonderful insight into our parent's relationship. We laughed, we cried, and we drank a lot of wine. I thought we knew them so well. We were wrong.

I hesitated to write in this journal. It seemed like an invasion of their privacy, but Michael convinced me it was only right to complete the story.

This will be the final entry. After today, I will tuck these pages back into Jacob's box of hugs and kisses. It is the perfect resting place for it. Perhaps someday our children will read these words and gain the same inspiration of love and spirit that Michael and I have.

Dad passed away a short three months after Mom died. Dr. Hardy told us he suffered from a massive heart attack in his sleep. He assured us that he didn't suffer. I don't doubt that it was an accurate medical diagnosis. However, I know the truth. Dad died of a broken heart.

Dad merely existed after Mom passed away. With her gone, he lost his purpose for living. It is simple. Without Maggie, there could be no John.

We will miss them for the rest of our lives. Yet, I take comfort in the knowledge that they are together again. And that is how it should be. Our family will always be blessed with the memories they have so graciously shared with us.

I feel safer knowing that our family is protected by two very special angels. I can feel the warmth of their presence as I write these words.

~

Dear Mom and Dad,

Thank you for your wonderful gift of love. We will treasure it forever. Once you mentioned that you believed this experience brought us closer. Truer words have never been spoken. Together, we have shared the greatest pain a family could endure. However, we have also shared the greatest joy.

You have taught us so much about life and love. We will carry your lessons with us forever. We are a part of you, and now it falls on our shoulders to carry on your legacy of love. It is an awesome responsibility, but one you have prepared us for.

I promise, we will live each day to its fullest. We will walk barefoot in the grass and we will lie beneath a star filled sky. We will take the time to really listen to a child speak. We won't hesitate to laugh and we won't be afraid to cry.

Most of all, we will never take love for granted. We will treasure it and hold it dear. All of this we will do, because of the wisdom you have shared with us.

Through the ages, there have been a million love stories written. But the greatest of all, will remain unknown, except to just a few.

It is the story of Maggie and John.

www.ingramcontent.com/pod-product-compliance
Lightning Source LLC
Chambersburg PA
CBHW030531030726
47495CB00004B/950